The smell of a Thanksgiving feast filled the house.

Lauren hurried to the kitchen, but just enough cooking time remained for the dressing and rolls. Nick hovered at her elbow, sneaking bites of everything as it cooked, until finally, she shooed him out of her kitchen.

Lauren glanced toward the dining room where Nick stood, puzzling over what piece of her grandmother's silverware went where. Her heart filled to bursting point with love. How thankful she was for him on this day meant for thanks. He'd brought sunshine into her life. He'd brought rain. He'd taught her how to treasure both.

How could she let him ride off into the colorful western sunset...alone?

Linda Varner brings you the joy of the holiday season with three very special couples who discover a HOME FOR THE HOLIDAYS...and forever.

WON'T YOU BE MY HUSBAND? (11/96)
MISTLETOE BRIDE (12/96)
NEW YEAR'S WIFE (1/97)

Dear Reader,

In Arlene James's *Desperately Seeking Daddy*, a harried, single working mom of three feels like Cinderella at the ball when Jack Tyler comes into her life. He wins over her kids, charms her mother and sets straight her grumpy boss. He's the FABULOUS FATHER of her kids' dreams—and the husband of hers!

Although the BUNDLE OF JOY in Amelia Varden's arms is not her natural child, she's loved the baby boy from birth. And now one man has come to claim her son—and her heart—in reader favorite Elizabeth August's *The Rancher and the Baby*.

Won't You Be My Husband? begins Linda Varner's trilogy HOME FOR THE HOLIDAYS, in which a woman ends up engaged to be married after a ten-minute reunion with a bad-boy hunk!

What's a smitten bookkeeper to do when her gorgeous boss asks her to be his bride—even for convenience? Run down the aisle!...in DeAnna Talcott's *The Bachelor and the Bassinet*.

In Pat Montana's *Storybook Bride*, tight-lipped rancher Kody Sanville's been called a half-breed his whole life and doesn't believe in storybook anything. So why can't he stop dreaming of being loved by Becca Covington?

Suzanne McMinn makes her **debut** with *Make Room for Mommy*, in which a single woman with motherhood and marriage on her mind falls for a single dad who isn't at all interested in saying "I do"...or so he thinks!

From classic love stories, to romantic comedies to emotional heart tuggers, Silhouette Romance offers six wonderful new novels each month by six talented authors. I hope you enjoy all six books this month—and every month.

Regards,

Melissa Senate,
Senior Editor

Please address questions and book requests to:
Silhouette Reader Service
U.S.: 3010 Walden Ave., P.O. Box 1325, Buffalo, NY 14269
Canadian: P.O. Box 609, Fort Erie, Ont. L2A 5X3

WON'T YOU BE MY HUSBAND?

Linda Varner

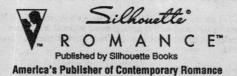

Silhouette®
R O M A N C E™
Published by Silhouette Books
America's Publisher of Contemporary Romance

To my special friend, Tammie Burgess,
a cosmetologist with talent, skill
and a heart of gold.

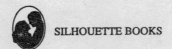 SILHOUETTE BOOKS

ISBN 0-373-19188-X

WON'T YOU BE MY HUSBAND?

Copyright © 1996 by Linda Varner Palmer

This edition published by arrangement with Harlequin Books S.A.

Printed in U.S.A.

Books by Linda Varner

Silhouette Romance

Heart of the Matter #625
Heart Rustler #644
The Luck of the Irish #665
Honeymoon Hideaway #698
Better To Have Loved #734
A House Becomes a Home #780
Mistletoe and Miracles #835
As Sweet as Candy #851
Diamonds Are Forever #868
A Good Catch #906
Something Borrowed #943
Firelight and Forever #966
*Dad on the Job #1036
*Believing in Miracles #1051
*Wife Most Unlikely #1068
†Won't You Be My Husband? #1088

*Mr. Right, Inc.
†Home for the Holidays

LINDA VARNER

confesses she is a hopeless romantic. Nothing is more thrilling, she believes, than the battle of wits between a man and a woman who are meant for each other but just don't know it yet! Linda enjoys writing romance and considers herself very lucky to have been both a RITA finalist and a third-place winner in the National Readers' Choice Awards in 1993.

A full-time federal employee, Linda lives in Arkansas with her husband and their two children. She loves to hear from readers and you can write to her at 813 Oak St., Suite 10A-277, Conway, AR 72032.

Recipe for A Wonderful Thanksgiving

1 teenage "bad boy" (complete with motorcycle)

1 kid sister (not the bad boy's)

1 chance meeting

1 make-believe engagement

Mix together the first two ingredients. Set aside to age. Several years later, toss in a chance meeting. Add the make-believe engagement, then heat to boiling point.

Yield: *A Home for the Holidays... and forever!*

Chapter One

"Well, if it isn't Sissy West. My, how you've grown."

Lauren West started at the sound of the husky, masculine drawl and looked up at its owner, standing in front of her in the hot dog line, his back now to their destination. She saw a ruggedly handsome face and finger-combed black hair. She saw glittering brown eyes fringed with thick dark lashes. She saw the sexiest smile in the state of Texas, maybe the world....

She saw a stranger. A lean, six-foot-and-more stranger, who somehow knew a nickname she'd worked years to lose.

"H-haven't I though?" Lauren stammered, smiling politely at the man even as her brain flipped frantically through mug shots of long-lost relatives, old boyfriends and past patients of her physician father.

"You don't have a clue who I am, do you?"

So much for fooling the guy. Lauren hesitated, then gave in to honesty. "Sorry, no."

"Nicolas Gatewood."

Nicolas Gatewood? Ex-beau of big sister Diana? Texas City bad boy? High school dropout? Lauren's gaze swept down and then back up his athletic frame, looking for any of Nick Gatewood's trademarks: boots, black leather jacket or the words *Harley-Davidson*. Instead she saw a navy blue cotton sweater, faded form-fitting jeans and scruffy loafers.

"You're lying," she blurted, an answer that made him roar with laughter. That joyous sound turned the heads of the Dallas Cowboy football fans lined up all around them. Lauren didn't care. That laugh also confirmed the man's claim. Only one male alive displayed mirth with such abandon, and it was with difficulty that she hid her pleasure at seeing him again.

"I'm not, and I can prove it." He thought for a moment. "Close your eyes and picture the corner of Third Street and Marshall, Texas City, Texas, on a sunny May afternoon about...oh...nineteen or twenty years ago. There are lots of kids standing around waiting for the school bus. One of them is a thirteen-year-old squirt of a tomboy with curly blond hair, freckles and knobby knees." He paused. "Get the picture so far?"

"It's slowly coming into focus." Actually the scene was crystal clear, but Lauren didn't tell Nick that. Why, she wasn't sure, but guessed it had something to do with his blatant masculinity, his utter self-confidence, his charm.

Or was it the fact that the longer he talked, the longer she got to stare at him?

"The tomboy, we'll call her Sissy, is being mercilessly teased by three high schoolers—"

"Moe, Larry and Curly," Lauren wryly supplied.

Nick grinned. "She's frightened, near tears."

"Bull. She's about to break Moe's nose."

Nick's grin widened. "So you remember that afternoon?"

"Of course I remember it. You saved those idiots from a thrashing they would never have forgotten."

"And all this time I thought it was *you* I saved when I rode up on my trusty steed."

"Trusty steed, my foot. You rode up on that beat-up Harley of yours, and the only reason I got on behind you was pity."

He frowned slightly. "You felt sorry for me? Why?"

"Diana had just dumped you for Brent McEntyre, remember?" Lauren's four-years-older sister had loved 'em and left 'em at an alarming rate during her teenage years.

"Ach. So she had. I'd forgotten."

I'll bet. Lauren still remembered the look on Nick's face when he'd dropped her off at her house moments after the rescue and found Brent's sports car parked in the drive. *Devastated* didn't begin to describe his expression. "That's the last time I ever saw you."

"Until now."

"Yes, until now." Lauren smiled at him and, suddenly self-conscious, tried to play it cool as she twisted a tendril of hair that had escaped from the French twist at the back of her head. The next second she abandoned that and, with a hearty "God, it's great to see you!" threw her arms around his middle.

Nick hugged her back so hard the breath left her lungs in a soft whoosh. Just as abruptly he let go and glanced over his shoulder to check his progress in the concession line. He moved a few steps closer to the counter, then gave Lauren his attention again.

"I'm surprised to see you here," he said, stuffing the tips of his fingers in the front pockets of his jeans. She realized then that he didn't look totally at ease, himself. "I seem to recall that you hate football."

Lauren shrugged casually even as she noted the slight flush now staining his tanned cheeks. Had the hug embarrassed him or did he, too, want it to go on forever?

"One of my partners had a spare ticket."

"Partners? What are you...a lawyer or something?"

She laughed. "Or something. I'm a doctor—OB-GYN." She told him the names of her four female partners and where their clinic was located.

Nick slapped the palm of one hand to his head as though pronouncing himself a dunce. "I should've guessed you'd follow in the old man's footsteps. You had his knack for healing hurts even when you were a kid."

Lauren thought of her father, a general practitioner dead eleven years. "You think?"

"I know." Nick glanced back to check his progress in the line once again and adjusted his position accordingly. Lauren followed suit, keeping the distance between them the same. "You live here in Irving?"

"Dallas, actually. What about you? What are you doing now and where?"

"I'm an architect." He laughed at her startled expression "With Avery, Sanders and Wright, Inc. Heard of them?"

Still stunned by his occupation—as far as she knew the man had never finished high school—Lauren barely managed a nod. Who hadn't heard of the prestigious firm?

"I work in Dallas, too," Nick said, adding, as if to answer her unspoken questions, "G.E.D. in the Army, college after I got out."

"Why, that's wonderful!" Lauren exclaimed, giving him both a verbal and literal pat on the back.

"You're surprised, aren't you?"

"To be honest, I am."

"You thought I'd wind up working in a garage somewhere, wearing grease-stained coveralls and a torn T-shirt."

"That's not true," Lauren retorted even though she knew he teased. For some reason it was important that Nick understand she'd always thought he had potential. "I may not have guessed you'd be an architect, but I knew you'd go places."

"Oh, I went places, all right—beginning with boot camp and ending up in Germany. Six countries in seven years."

"Must have been exciting," Lauren murmured, nudging him to close the gap in the line again.

Nick moved obediently. "Turned my life around. Taught me discipline. Gave me pride, goals. Enlisting was the best decision I ever made."

"An architect..." Lauren shook her head, still not quite believing it. "So are you happily married now, with two-point-five children?"

"Not me." He glanced at her left hand, obviously looking for a wedding band. His eyes widened in surprise. "You're single, too?"

"Yes, and probably always will be unless you know a saint who wouldn't mind his wife delivering everyone's babies but her own...."

"*Hey, Bud! Do you want a dog or not?*"

Thus alerted that he was holding up the line again, Nick said, "Don't run off," then turned his back on her.

Lauren noted that he was just two people from the counter now. Guessing he'd face forward until served, she made the most of the opportunity to examine this view of him. *Not bad,* she thought, relishing how his sweater accentuated his broad shoulders and how his jeans hugged his backside and long legs. Clearly he hadn't let his desk job get the best of his physique. No, a man had to stay active to maintain a body like that.

"Lauren? Dr. Lauren West?"

For the second time that afternoon a man called her name. This time, however, Lauren recognized the voice. She cringed.

"It *is* you!" Frank Montgomery, friend of Lauren's brother-in-law, exclaimed as he angled up from nowhere and turned her around to face him. "And looking h-o-t as ever. How've you been, babe?"

"Fine," Lauren replied, unsuccessfully ducking the wet kiss he planted right on her mouth. That kiss brought back vivid memories of their one and only date in Houston last month—a disaster from the get-go, thanks to his inflated ego, ever-ready lips and busy, busy hands.

Frank, who stood maybe an inch over her own five-feet-eight, lay a heavy arm across her shoulders, holding her so that her back was to the food counter and the scoop neck of her sweater in his direct line of vision.

"Would you believe I was going to call you after the game today? I'm in town until Wednesday. Thought we could get together and take up—" he gave her arm a promising squeeze "—where we left off."

Though tempted to slap the man senseless, Lauren kept her cool. Frank Montgomery was, after all, head of the surgery department at the hospital where Diana's physician husband, Stephen, hoped to earn operating room privileges. Diana would kill Lauren if she did anything to jeopardize his chances.

"I really can't—" Lauren murmured, trying to ease free of his embrace without giving him a peek at her breasts.

"Playing hard to get?" His beer-scented whisper fanned the tendrils of hair framing Lauren's face. His lips loomed inches from her own.

"I'm not playing at all...."

"Lauren, honey, do you want mustard or ketchup on your—er, sorry, didn't mean to *interrupt.*" It was Nick, and looking as dangerous as 007 ever did.

Oh so grateful he'd saved Frank from bodily harm, Lauren wrenched herself free and followed his inspired lead. "Don't be absurd," she murmured, pulling her sweater back up on her bare shoulder. "This is just Frank Montgomery, whom I met through Stephen a few weeks ago. Frank, this is Nicolas Gatewood, my—"

"Fiancé," Nick interjected, extending his right hand, which a visibly flustered—or was he angry?—Frank took, shook and quickly released.

"S-Stephen is going to be on the surgical staff at Houston Regional just as soon as his appointment is approved," Lauren stammered, still trying to adjust to Nick's sudden conversion from *friend* to *fiancé.* "Frank, here, is head of the department." Anxiously, Lauren searched Nick's expression for any sign that he understood her unspoken message: be nice to this jerk.

Nick's quick wink, which could not have been seen by their companion, told her that he did. "Houston Regional's gain."

"Uh, yes, of course," Frank murmured. "Stephen is a fine surgeon." Lauren noted that his gaze dropped to her left hand just as Nick's had earlier. He frowned ever so slightly. "How long have you two been engaged?"

"Not long at all," Nick replied when words failed Lauren.

"We, um, haven't even had a chance to shop for a diamond," she added, trying to assuage the doubt she read in Frank's expression.

"I...see. Well, congratulations and best of luck." He began to edge away.

"Thanks," Nick replied, standing by Lauren's side until the man slithered off into the crowd. At that point he glanced back toward the counter. "Rescuing damsels in distress is not without its price."

"What...?" Lauren, still in a bit of a daze, frowned after Frank.

"I lost my place in line, and not even for bratwurst on a roll will I go to the back and start over."

A quick glance toward the head of the line confirmed it. "Oh, gosh, I'm sorry. Are you very hungry?"

"My stomach is gnawing my backbone."

"I have a chocolate bar in my purse."

"Give it to me, oh bride-to-be," Nick told her, holding out his hand, palm upwards and grinning like the Cheshire Cat.

Abruptly Lauren grabbed Nick's hand and as good as dragged him away from the crowded concession area to the edge of the walkway. "I can't believe you told Frank that we're engaged."

"Got rid of him, didn't it?"

"Yes, but..."

"And probably for good."

"Probably, but..."

"Then how about a little appreciation?"

Lauren sighed and gave him the credit he surely deserved. "Thanks, Nick. I owe you."

"One good turn *does* deserve another," Nick agreed, leaning against a concrete support, arms crossed over his chest. "You can pay your bill October twelfth at my boss's house."

"Excuse me?"

"I have a dinner party to go to a week from Wednesday. I want you to go, too, and play fiancée the way I just did."

"You can't be serious."

"Never more."

"But why?"

"So a certain someone will keep her hands to herself."

Lauren laughed in utter disbelief. "Can't you just tell her to cool it?"

"I'm afraid it's not that simple."

"Who *is* this mystery lady, for crying out loud?" Lauren teased, enjoying Nick's obvious discomfort at having to admit his problem. "The boss's wife?"

"Exactly."

Lauren's jaw dropped. "You're kidding."

"Wish I were. Will you help me?"

"I don't know if this is such a good idea. Won't there be complications at your office? I mean, your boss will surely spread the word. Telling a white lie to Frank, who, with luck, I'll never see again, is one thing. Telling one to your co-workers is quite another. Won't they wonder if they don't see us out together now and then?"

"I rarely socialize with my co-workers, so I seldom see them anywhere besides the office. If I do, I'll just tell them you're delivering a baby or something." He took both her hands in his. "So can you do it?" he asked, flashing her a killer smile.

Lauren sighed and gave up the ghost. Freeing her hands, she dug in her purse for her pocket calendar. A quick peek at it revealed she could probably manage a dinner party in ten days. "I can do it, and I will—"

"Thanks, Sissy."

"—on the condition that you never, ever call me *that* again."

"Agreed...Dr. West. Now dinner is at eight. I'll pick you up at seven-thirty."

"Okay." Lauren dropped the calendar in her purse, then dug around for one of her personal cards, which she handed to him, along with a slightly squashed chocolate bar. "Here's my address. There's my home phone number. Is this thing dressy?"

"Dressy enough. I have to wear a tie." He looked as if the thought choked him as much as the tie would.

Lauren laughed, pleased to see that a little of the old Nick still lurked inside the new. Not that there was one thing wrong with the new Nick. She found the combination of the past and present a most tempting package.

But who had time for temptation? Certainly not Lauren, who was suddenly assailed with second thoughts about the wisdom of all this. As if reading them, Nick frowned.

"You're not going to back out on me, are you?"

"No," Lauren heard herself say. "This is a debt of honor, after all, and I—oops!" Her pager, clipped out of sight on the waistband of her jeans before she left for the stadium that morning, vibrated against her skin. With a sigh, Lauren raised the hem of her sweater and pressed a button to illuminate the number of her paging service. ''Must be a real problem for them to page me here. I'm on fifth call today.''

''*Fifth* call? What in the heck is that?''

''It's a rather complicated on-call system my partners and I worked out to keep our patients happy. Most of them are . . . hmm, I'm not sure how to put this . . .''

''Filthy rich?''

Lauren laughed. ''I was going to say spoiled rotten, but filthy rich is appropriate, too. Anyway, to make sure every patient gets immediate and personal attention, my partners and I rotate responsibility. First call gets called first. Second call gets called if the doctor on first call is already busy. Third call—''

Nick held up his hands as if warding off a blow. ''I get the picture, I get the picture. And I'm wondering 'who's on first'?''

''Dr. Carmencita Renfroe has first call tonight,'' Lauren replied, only belatedly realizing Nick referred to the classic Abbott and Costello routine and not her equally complicated call schedule. She stuck out her tongue at him, an action that won her his mischievous grin. ''I really have to go.''

''Not before we shake on this engagement thing.'' Nick reached for her hand, but instead of a shake, he gave it a kiss . . . right in the sweaty palm. Lauren's heart screeched to a halt then jump started back to life. She snatched her hand away and swiped it down her jeans.

''Just what was that?'' she demanded, feigning indignation. It wouldn't do for him to know just how much she wished that kiss had landed on her lips instead of in her hand.

''Inexcusable,'' Nick said with a decidedly sheepish smile. ''Just because I'm already half in lust with you is no excuse for me to act like Frank. I'm sorry, and I promise I won't ever do it again."

"Oh, you don't have to go *that* far," Lauren thoughtlessly blurted out even as she registered his "half in lust" comment. Too late she heard the echo of her own candid reply. "What I mean is, I'd never compare you to Frank. You two aren't a bit alike."

"That's true. I'm an architect—he's a doctor."

Lauren blinked at that response. Did Nick mean he considered them alike in ways other than professional? she instantly wondered. Like, maybe, sexual...?

Half in lust.

The very concept took her breath away, probably because Lauren was already half—if not three-fourths—*in lust* with him, too.

Amazing what a few years of growing up could do.

She swallowed hard, suddenly as rattled as a teenager on a first date, even though she was as experienced as two serious affairs could leave her.

"Now I'll be out of touch for a few days," Nick said. "But I'll call your secretary early next week to have her remind you about our date, okay?"

"Okay," she told him, though the chances of her forgetting were slim and none. "I really have to go, Nick." With a wave, she spun on her heel and tried to put some distance between them.

"Lauren?"

"What?" She paused but did not dare turn to look at him again.

"Who the hell is Stephen?"

Lauren smiled to herself. "Diana's husband, Stephen Bayer."

"So he's family," Nick murmured, softly adding, "Good," a word that Lauren barely heard; a word that did not give her peace of mind . . . or body.

True to his word, Nick called Lauren's office the day of the dinner party and asked for her secretary. After identifying himself, he explained that he was an *old friend* of Dr. West's who wanted to remind her about a social commitment.

"You don't sound *old*," replied the young woman, who called herself Lisa.

Nick heard her playful tone and grinned, liking her on the spot. "Must be the connection. You don't sound a day over twenty-one, yourself."

"I'm *not* a day over twenty-one," she retorted with a laugh. "I am old enough to take a message, however. What do you want me to put in this one?"

Nick grinned a little bigger. "Just remind Dr. West that she has a date with me tonight at seven-thirty."

"Did you say . . . a date?" Lisa sounded as if the concept were a new one.

"A date. You do know what one of those is, don't you?"

"I certainly do," she replied, somewhat hesitantly adding, "Though I'm not at all sure Dr. West does."

Her casual comment stayed on Nick's mind all day. Lauren didn't date? Unbelievable! Was she too busy? Too tired? Too picky?

Couldn't be *picky,* Nick thought with a dry laugh as he drove his sleek silver Mercedes-Benz to Lauren's Dallas neighborhood that night. He glanced at his gold wristwatch, purchased with money from his first Avery, Sanders and Wright, Inc. paycheck some four years ago. Remembering how he'd passed over a style he liked better so he could purchase the most expensive one in the jewelry store, he noted the time, 7:15, and shook his head. Thank goodness money had finally lost its hold on him. It had taken a couple of years—the scars of poverty ran deep—but now he could honestly say he knew what was important.

Lauren, for example. Seeing her at the stadium was a gift from the gods that Nick did not deserve, but accepted. And though certain he would one day rue their meeting—like when her class act saw through the sham of his nouveau respectability—at the moment he was grateful for the diversion.

A glance at the card Lauren had given Nick reminded him for what address he now searched: 14 Blue Moon Lane. He spotted the street just ahead and, shortly after, her house, a modest two-story brick with a neatly manicured lawn. Turning into the drive, situated midpoint in a curve he considered dangerous, Nick braked his car and killed the engine, then got out and walked to Lauren's front door.

He raised his hand to ring the bell, but hesitated, suddenly nervous. What the hell? he wondered, trying to analyze this unexpected reluctance to see Lauren again.

Was it concern he would do something stupid tonight that kept his hand hovering inches from the bell? Or was it worry he would put his foot in his mouth? Both, Nick instantly realized . . . plus raw fear that he hadn't imagined the spark of interest he saw in her eye. That he would respond to it and reveal just how incredibly, sexually attracted he was to her, too.

Damn, but she was a beauty. Tall, generously curved, graceful. He broke out into a cold sweat just remembering how she'd looked Sunday in tight jeans, leather knee boots and that sweater . . . dear heaven, that sweater.

Nick swallowed hard. The door suddenly swung open.

"Are you going to stand there all night or ring the bell?" Lauren demanded, hands on hips.

"I-it's broken," Nick lied, for lack of a better excuse for loitering like an idiot on her front porch.

"It is not," Lauren retorted, reaching out to thumb the button. At once chimes sounded inside the house. "So what's the real problem?"

"I'm, uh, early." He glanced at his watch, noting with relief that he was, indeed, early—one minute and thirty seconds.

"That's okay. I'm ready." Laughing, clearly not fooled by Nick's fibs, though she couldn't possibly know the reason for them, Lauren stepped back and ushered him into the house. "So what do you think?" she demanded, throwing out her arms as if to encompass her whole house in a hug.

"I think you look like a million dollars," Nick replied, even though he knew she wanted his opinion of the house, not her person. His hungry gaze devoured Lauren, savoring every inch of her from auburn curls to open-toed high heels. His heart turned a back flip. His knees threatened to give way.

"Not me, doofus," she said. "My house. Do you like it?"

"It's incredible," he murmured, without dragging his gaze away from her glittery black dress. Cut in a style from the past, its padded shoulders, diamond cutout neck, and knee-length skirt accentuated her shapely figure and drove his pulse to triple digits.

"I rented it three months ago with the option to buy and have been working like crazy decorating ever since. Only the bedroom is finished. I know we need to be going, but would you like to come up and look at it?"

She wanted him in her bedroom? Dazed by his good fortune, Nick followed her up the stairs. He noted that Lauren had to grasp a handful of skirt, thereby widening the slit in back, so she could manage the steps.

"I have the most gorgeous bedroom suite in the world."

And the best legs, Nick silently added, relishing the tantalizing lengths of limb Lauren unwittingly revealed. Though tempted to hang back a step or two, he resisted. It wouldn't do for her to catch him trying to get a glimpse of her panties. As it was, he'd have to keep his jacket buttoned all night to hide his unfortunate physical reaction to the seams of her sexy black stockings.

Lauren took a right at the top of the carpeted stair, leading Nick into a bedroom that looked as if it had come straight from "Lifestyles of the Rich and Famous."

"My God," he murmured, momentarily distracted from Lauren, herself. Slowly he turned, taking in every detail of the cream-colored furniture, the diaphanous cream-colored curtains, the plush cream-colored carpet. The only color in the room besides cream, cream, cream was a splash of burnished gold here and there, the red roses he'd sent her on Monday and, at the moment, Lauren, herself, dressed as she was in take-no-prisoners black.

"You don't like it."

"It's...incredible. I feel as if I've stepped into a fairy tale. All that's missing is the virgin princess, stretched out on that four-poster bed, waiting to be kissed awake by the handsome prince."

"Princess, heck! This is *my* room. Therefore, *I'm* the one who gets the kiss."

"Then all I can say is 'Look out, Sleeping Beauty,' because if you're wearing that dress when the prince shows up, you won't be a virgin for long."

"Oh, I took care of that little problem years ago," Lauren told him with an airy wave of her hand. She walked over to the cheval mirror and smoothed her dress down over her hips. "So you like the outfit?"

"It's really beautiful."

"Why, thank you."

"You're welcome..." *To my sex—to my heart—to my life.* Hearing the echo of his unspoken offer, Nick tensed. It would be easy to get in over his head, here. So easy.

"What's wrong?" asked Lauren, who now stood close enough to feel the reaction.

"I was just wondering where you're going to clip your pager," Nick quickly lied. While he didn't mind her knowing he found her desirable tonight, he had no intentions of admitting he'd actually, even for a millisecond, thought of her in conjunction with his tomorrows. That was an insanity he could neither explain nor understand, unless seeing her again had somehow resurrected long-buried dreams of the good life. Too bad that Nicolas Gatewood, more than anyone, knew the good life wasn't for everyone. "Assuming you're taking it with you."

"Of course I'm taking it with me. And I'm putting it in your shirt pocket." Lauren scooped up her purse, took out the pager and tucked it in his shirt pocket. Then she smoothed his shirt and tie. "Goodness, but you're all tensed up," she murmured, the next instant stepping behind Nick and gently kneading his shoulders. "Take off your jacket."

"What for?"

"Your muscles are in knots." Even through the fabric of his black jacket and snow-white shirt, her probing fingers seared his flesh. "They need attention."

I'll show you a muscle that needs attention! Nick's libido screamed, further rattling his shaky nerves. "Though I appreciate the offer, we really don't have time for a back rub, Lauren. We have to be at Phillip Avery's in—" he glanced at his watch, noting that his hands...hell, his whole body...trembled at her touch "—twenty minutes, and it's going to take every one of them to get there."

"Then I'll give you a rain check," Lauren murmured, tugging playfully on his earlobe.

Nick jumped as if she'd goosed him.

"Are you sure you're all right?" Lauren demanded. Serious now, and obviously concerned, she raised his left arm and ducked under it to stand eyes-to-Adam's-apple with him.

"I guess I am a little nervous about this dinner party. I'm not sure of the reason for it. And then there's this phony engagement business. Speaking of which—" Nick dug into his jacket pocket and retrieved the tiny blue velvet box he'd tucked there earlier "—put this on."

Wide-eyed with curiosity, Lauren opened the box. While she examined the diamond solitaire inside, Nick examined her and saw the stuff of which a bad boy's dreams were made: auburn hair, big blue eyes, kissable lips. *Man, oh man.*

She was out of his league and always had been. Yet here they stood—face-to-face and, of all things, faking an engagement.

"Where'd you get this?" Lauren held the ring up under his nose.

"My fiancée."

"You've been engaged?"

"That's right."

"What happened?"

"Every time she set the wedding date, I found an excuse to change it."

"Tsk. Tsk. And how many times did this happen?"

"Four."

"No wonder she gave the ring back to you."

"Actually, she *threw* it back to me, and I never blamed her."

To Nick's relief, Lauren slipped the ring on her finger instead of asking any more questions about that painful period in his past. "It's a little loose, but I promise I won't lose it."

"Lose it. Lose it!" Ready to escape Lauren's pristine bedroom, Nick walked out the door and down the hall to the stairs. Lauren turned off the light and joined him. Together they descended into the foyer, where she retrieved her coat from a closet. Moments after, they left the house.

The clock on the dash said 8:10 when Nick braked to a halt in Phillip Avery's circle drive and assisted Lauren from the car. They hurried up the steps to the house, Lauren exclaiming over everything from the massive oak trees to the antique mailbox. It warmed Nick's heart to hear her comments. Although a noted obstetrician in one of the city's most influential clinics—at least according to the secretary who'd ordered the roses for him—Lauren was still just Sissy West from a small Texas town on the Gulf of Mexico.

Incredible, that, and disconcertingly appealing.

"Do *I* need to ring the bell?" Lauren asked, no doubt referring to his earlier reluctance to ring hers.

"Feel free."

Lauren reached up, then slowly lowered her hand. "Do you really think they'll believe we're in love, Nick? I mean, we didn't practice or anything—"

"Trust me, Lauren," Nick couldn't resist teasing. "If I'd had the slightest idea you wanted to practice loving me, I'd have been over every night this week."

Chapter Two

"Why, Nick Gatewood, shame on you!" Laughing over her case of nerves, Lauren punched the doorbell. She heard its ring, muted by the heavy front door. Then the ornate wooden barrier was flung open wide.

"Hello, Nicky," crooned an emerald-eyed brunette Lauren guessed to be in her early twenties. She included Lauren in her smile almost as an afterthought. "Please come in."

Grateful when Nick took her hand and led the way, Lauren stepped into the massive foyer of a house that could have been Tara, just as its mistress could have been Scarlett.

Unfortunately the conservatively attired man Lauren saw hurrying down the hall toward them couldn't have been Rhett. No, he more resembled Scarlett's father, a fact that explained Sabrina's attraction to Nick—who could claim more than a few Rhett-ly qualities.

Nick cleared his throat, transporting Lauren back to Texas from civil-war Georgia. "I'd like to introduce my fiancée, Lauren West, an obstetrician who works at a clinic here in town. Lauren, this is Phillip Avery, one of the cofounders of Avery, Sanders and Wright, and his wife, Sabrina."

"Fiancée? Well, I'll be damned," responded Phillip, with a delighted grin. He reached for Lauren's hand and pumped it vigorously up and down. "When did all this happen?"

"Just what I was about to ask," interjected Sabrina, her smile long since vanished, her skin tone as green as her eyes.

"It happened Sunday before last, actually," Nick replied, laying his left arm casually over Lauren's shoulders and pulling her closer to his side. Lauren slipped her arms around his waist and rested her cheek on his shoulder.

"We've known each other since we were teenagers," she said. "So naturally we were both surprised when our friendship blossomed into love."

Sabrina made a choking sound, which turned into a cough.

"Are you all right, darling?" Phillip asked, reaching out to pat her on the back.

"Fine," she snapped, shaking off his solicitous touch. Her venomous gaze nailed Lauren to the wall, or would have if Nick hadn't stepped in the line of fire. Lauren didn't know if he did it on purpose, but appreciated the gesture.

"We aren't ready to announce the engagement to everyone yet," Nick then said. "But we did want you two to know."

"We're honored to be some of the chosen few," Phillip told him, clearly oblivious to his wife's reaction. "And I think this wonderful news deserves a toast. Follow me." That said, the portly architect led the way into the den. An elaborate wet bar covered one wall, a massive fireplace, another. The third and fourth were made up of floor-to-ceiling shelves filled with books that Lauren bet the lady of the house had never dusted, much less read.

Phillip handed everyone a wineglass, into which he poured a measure of sparkling pink champagne, talking all the while. "I have to admit that lately I've been worried about Nick, who is the most gifted architect I've ever known, by the way."

Nick flushed crimson in response to the praise and avoided Lauren's gaze.

"He seemed restless," Phillip continued. "A bit down. In fact, I actually wondered if he was going to come back after his vacation in a couple of weeks. I guess I can quit worrying about that now."

"Yes, you can," Lauren murmured with a questioning glance at Nick. His expression told her nothing.

Moments later, drinks in hand, the four of them toasted an engagement as fake as Sabrina Avery's beauty mark. They next exchanged enough small talk to satisfy Phillip's curiosity about Lauren. Their young hostess then excused herself to the kitchen to check on the meal, sweetly inviting Lauren to come along.

"If I'm not back in ten minutes, call 911," Lauren whispered to Nick, under the guise of kissing his cheek. His eyes danced in response, and she saw a smile tugging the corners of his lips.

So he was enjoying this, huh? Well, no wonder. *She* was the one about to face the firing squad.

Lauren found the kitchen as impressive as the rest of the house and was surprised to discover that Sabrina seemed to know her way around the room.

"Something smells wonderful," Lauren murmured, trying, for the sake of Nick's career, to be friendly with this woman-child.

"It's an old family recipe. My parents own a restaurant in New York. They feature European cuisine. I was practically raised in the kitchen." She lifted the lid of a large, stainless steel pot and stirred the contents with a wooden spoon, releasing more aromatic steam. "Do you cook?"

"Not much," Lauren admitted without thought.

"Poor Nicky," murmured Sabrina. "He loves my cooking, you know." She replaced the lid on the cook pot and turned to face Lauren. "You've known him how long, did you say?"

"At least twenty-five years." *Which is a couple of years longer than you've been alive, sweetheart.*

"When is the wedding?"

"We're not sure yet, since we both have such busy schedules."

"May I give you a word of advice?"

A word of advice? From a preschooler? Though Lauren knew Sabrina's action resulted from her immaturity and jealousy, she barely managed to contain her sarcasm when she replied, "I'm all ears."

"My husband may not be particularly intuitive, but he is right about one thing. Nicky only pretends he is satisfied with his life." Sabrina tossed her long dark hair, then lifted her chin, her gaze arrogant and disdainful. "He's a rebel—a reckless, restless rebel—who will one day run away from everything, including you."

Lauren abruptly lost her battle with her own good manners. "Your point?"

"Enjoy him while you have him."

"Oh, but I do," Lauren replied, by now sick of the woman's melodrama and oddly disturbed by it. "In fact, that's why we were late tonight... because we were *enjoying* each other so much." Lauren spun on her heel and exited the kitchen, but not before she saw Sabrina's jaw drop.

When Lauren burst into the den a second later, her eyes met Nick's across the room. He leapt to his feet, a sure sign her anger must be showing. Phillip, clearly confused by Nick's abrupt action, stood, too.

"Your headache must be worse," Nick said to Lauren, taking her arm.

"Much," Lauren told him through gritted teeth. "If I could just get some fresh air."

"Why don't you take her out in the garden?" Phillip suggested, clearly concerned. "You know the way, I believe. I'll call you when everything is ready."

"Thanks," Nick murmured, grasping Lauren by the wrist and nearly dragging her down the hall and out double glass doors into the garden. The October breeze was a welcome relief, instantly cooling Lauren's flaming temper. Cherishing the night sounds and garden smells, she let Nick lead her through the softly illuminated area to a covered bench swing.

"Speak to me," he said the moment they were settled.

"That woman is such a witch!" Lauren exploded. "Granted, she's a baby one, but what potential!" She gave him an edited account of her recent conversation with Sabrina, leaving out the woman's prediction that Nick would soon break from the confines of propriety.

He groaned in response to her confession. "You actually told her we were late because we were making love?"

"As good as."

"Damn, Lauren."

"I know . . . I know. It was a terribly childish thing to do." She shook her head in disbelief that she'd let Sabrina get to her that way. "I don't know what came over me. I hope you're not upset."

To Lauren's astonishment, the night rang with Nick's laughter. "Awed by your creativity, maybe, but not upset. Did you really think I would be?"

"I wasn't sure. I mean, she is the boss's wife."

"Yeah, poor guy," Nick murmured, instantly sobering.

"And I did tell her one heck of a whopper."

"The lie wasn't *that* big."

"Are you kidding? We haven't even kissed."

"We can remedy that easily enough." Nick surprised Lauren by turning slightly so he could pull her up tight against him. He then brushed his lips over hers in the lightest of touches, just enough to leave her begging for more.

"You call that a kiss?" Lauren heard herself blurt out. It had been too, too long since a man had held her this close. She couldn't resist prolonging the contact even though no good would come of it.

With a grunt of satisfaction that must have meant *no,* Nick pressed his mouth to hers again and proceeded to demonstrate exactly what he called a kiss.

Firmly, yet gently, his lips seduced. He teased, he tasted, he tantalized . . . without words urging Lauren to open her mouth and let him deepen the kiss. She did, then took control—slipping her tongue between his teeth, exploring, savoring.

The thunder of Lauren's heartbeat drowned the night sounds. Nick's musky cologne obscured the garden smells. She heard a soft moan—his or hers?—and sighed with regret when he dragged his mouth from hers.

"Woman, you are lethal," Nick whispered, trailing his lips across her cheek so he could nibble the supersensitive spot just under her earlobe. Lauren shivered in response to the caress.

"Me?" She tipped her head, making it easier for him to nuzzle her neck. "You're the one who's lethal, and if I'd had the faintest idea you could kiss like that, I'd have fought Diana for you."

Nick snorted and raised his head. "Get real. You were only thirteen."

"Just the right age to learn about the birds and the bees," Lauren replied. To her surprise, Nick held her away from him.

"Who *did* teach you about the birds and the bees?"

"Bobby Winfree when I was eighteen."

"That empty-headed jock?"

Lauren shrugged. "He may have been an intellectual lightweight, but his kisses sure made my heart go pitter-pat."

"And what about my kisses?" Nick asked. "Do they do anything to your heart?"

"What is this, true confessions?"

"I was just curious."

"Hmm. Well, I'll tell you what your kisses do to my heart after you tell me what mine do to yours."

"It's interesting you should mention that, because my heart is acting really weird right now."

"What do you mean 'really weird'?" At once all business, Dr. West pressed her palm to Nick's chest. She tensed, then remembered and bubbled with laughter. "That's not your heart, Nick. That's my pager. It vibrates when I'm getting a call."

With a grin that admitted he knew that already, Nick placed his hand over hers and pinned it against his shirt pocket. "I'm not letting you answer that, until I have your promise we can finish our cardiac comparison later."

"Trust me when I tell you the mood won't be the same," Lauren murmured with disgust. How many times had that stupid pager interrupted a tender moment during the last few years of med school, residency and practice? Hundreds? No, more like thousands... at least it felt that way sometimes.

"Nick? Lauren?" It was Phillip, standing at the French doors. "Sabrina tells me that dinner is ready."

"We were just coming in. Lauren's been paged." Nick got to his feet and tugged Lauren to hers. "Only a couple of hours more and this night will be over," he whispered.

And when it ends, so will our engagement, Lauren silently answered, not a bit surprised to find herself despondent at the thought. Nick wasn't the only one who'd felt restless of late. So had she, if the oft-verbalized concern of her co-workers was anything to go by.

But running into Nick at the stadium had changed all that. Suddenly energized and loving it, she could not bear to think what would happen once he exited her life again.

Lauren took care of the page with one quick phone call, and the four of them soon made their way to the dining room where waited a table set with delicate china and crystal. Wishing for pepperoni pizza and a cold beer, Nick assisted Lauren into her chair, then sat across the table from her.

Halfway through Sabrina Avery's exotic meal, Nick discovered just how much his and Lauren's garden escapade was going to cost him in peace of mind and body. He found himself eating automatically, one ear tuned to the conversation of his host, all his other senses focused on Lauren, smiling demurely at him from time to time.

He heard her easy laugh, felt when she crossed her long legs and accidentally nudged him, smelled her cologne. As for taste, even the highly spiced entrée did not obliterate his memory of the flavor that was so distinctly Lauren. His whole body felt charged up and ready—some parts more than others—and he squirmed in his chair like a little kid anxiously awaiting the dessert.

Thus distracted, he had little to say the rest of the evening, but if Phillip noticed, he did not comment. As for Sabrina, she said maybe three words all during dinner and after. Finally at ten-thirty Nick and Lauren murmured their thank-yous and goodbyes and escaped to the car.

"Am I to understand that the whole reason for this dinner tonight was so Phillip Avery could *hint* he would sponsor you, should one of the partners at Avery, Sanders and Wright decide to retire?" Lauren asked, once they were safely away. She had already taken off a shoe and was rubbing her foot as if it were hurting, a task for which Nick wished he could volunteer.

"Looks that way," he said, glancing over at her every time they passed under a streetlight. "Retirement rumors have been circulating around the office for months now, though no one has a clue which partner is retiring or who will be invited to replace him. I think this dinner tonight is Avery's way of saying he's sticking around and wants me in management.''

"Why, that would be fantastic!" Lauren exclaimed, the next instant adding, "Wouldn't it?" in a voice so uncertain Nick knew she must have picked up on his mood. It was oddly flat, considering partnership in the architectural firm had been a dream of his for years.

"Yeah, sure." To change the subject, he said, "Would a kiss make that better?"

"Would a...? Oh. My foot." She shook her head and slipped her shoe back on. "Doctor that I am, I can say with complete authority that it would not. A Band-Aid would do wonders, though."

"I have a whole tin of them at my place. Fluorescent ones. Want to take a detour and stop by there?"

For a moment Lauren didn't answer, then she turned slightly in the bucket seat as though to better see him, not easy since the streetlights had begun to thin. "Why do I get the feeling I've just been invited to your place to look at some etchings?"

"Because you have?"

Lauren sighed. "Nick, there's something I have to tell you—"

" 'No thanks'?" So the party was already over. Though disappointed, Nick wasn't surprised. He'd known it wouldn't take long for Beauty to tire of the Beast and honestly hadn't planned beyond tonight. "I understand, Lauren. I know I'm not your type, and I had no business even suggesting that we . . . um . . . get to know each other again."

"For your information, I don't have a type. And what I was going to say is this—while there's nothing I'd like better than to get to know you again, I've tried twice to evenly balance my personal life with my professional one, and I just can't seem to do it.''

"That's crazy. There must be thousands, maybe millions, of doctors who carry pagers and yet manage to balance their professional and personal lives.''

"I didn't say it couldn't be done, Nick. I said I couldn't do it *evenly* ... at least at this stage in my life. I've only been in private practice for two years. I have dues to pay. Therefore, much as I'd love to spend all my time getting to know you again, the most I can promise is leftovers.''

"I'd never ask for *all* your time, Lauren. In fact, I don't recall asking for any of it. I just thought—heck, I don't know what I thought.''

"That the kisses we shared tonight were incredible, maybe? That it felt really great to be held so tight?''

"That just about sums it up." Nick turned onto Blue Moon Lane, then a couple of blocks later, into her drive. He braked the car and killed the engine, then sat without speaking, not sure what to say to break the awkward silence between them.

Fortunately Lauren didn't have that problem. "Just so you know, I enjoyed our garden party, too.''

"Yeah?''

"Yeah.''

Nick shifted his position so he could see her better. "What would you say if I told you I want to kiss you again?''

Leaning to cover the distance between the bucket seats, she gave him a light peck on the mouth that instantly set him on fire for her. In a flash, Nick wrapped his arms around Lauren, holding her where she was—close, and in danger of being stabbed by the stick shift.

"Now what about our doing some serious making out? Would you go for that, too?"

"Not in this car, I won't," she answered, squirming to free herself. "And I guess you'd better define *serious*."

"Serious is—*jeez!*" Nick slapped a hand to his pocket, only then remembering that pesky pager, vibrating in his pocket like an angry bumblebee. With an embarrassed laugh, he handed the pager to Lauren, then flipped on the dome light so she could better view the number she needed to call.

"Lisa Millcott. One of our receptionists. I'd better call her, and I'd better set this pager to beep again." Lauren did so, then opened the car door and looked back at Nick, who had never moved. "You're coming in, aren't you?"

"You want me to?"

"How else will I ever discover what 'serious making out' is?" Laughing, she slipped from the car and ran across the dew-kissed lawn to her sidewalk. Nick battled his raging libido maybe half a second before he leapt from the car and loped after her. Together they climbed the porch steps. After digging into her bag, Lauren unlocked the front door and pushed it open. The ring of her telephone greeted them. Lauren dashed into her den, set her pager on an end table, then scooped up the telephone receiver.

"Hello?"

Nick, who'd followed Lauren into the room, saw her face light up. "Why, hi there." She covered the mouthpiece with one hand and whispered, "It's Diana," then motioned for him to have a seat on the blue chintz couch, which he did. She sank down on a matching chair, slipped out of her shoes and tucked one leg up under the other. "Is everyone okay? I mean, you're usually snoring by now." Lauren winked at Nick as though she knew that remark would bug the heck out of big sis.

Nick grinned, imagining Diana's rejoinder. He expected Lauren to laugh, but to his surprise he saw her jaw drop and her cheeks flame crimson.

"Di...please...let me explain—"

Lauren's gaze met Nick's across the room. She drew her forefinger across her neck, the age-old sign of disaster and certain doom.

"Yes, Frank *was* talking about the Nick Gatewood you once dated—"

Uh-oh.

"—but he didn't have his facts exactly straight." She shook her head, clearly agitated by whatever Diana had to say to that. "No, I'm not saying he lied. What I'm saying is...is..." Once again Lauren put her hand over the mouthpiece and gave Nick her attention. "What am I saying?"

"Depends on what *she's* saying," Nick retorted.

"Di's upset, and I mean really upset, because I told Frank about the engagement before I told her."

Great. "Then you'd better tell her the truth."

"Schoolgirl crush!" Lauren loudly exclaimed, apparently in response to something Diana said. Nick doubted she'd heard his suggestion at all. "You don't know what you're talking about. I never had any schoolgirl crush on Nick Gatewood." She positively glared at Nick as if he, and not her sister, were the accuser. "As for his suitability as a mate, I'll have you know that Nick is an architect. Yes, I said architect. He works at a very prestigious firm here in Dallas and is going to be offered a partnership very soon."

Nick groaned at that exaggeration, a sound that earned him another glare from Lauren.

"You're *what?* Oh, Di, I wish you wouldn't." Lauren flashed Nick a look of pure panic, but said nothing, clearly on the receiving end of a sisterly diatribe. "But of course I'd love to see you, it's just that I'm always on call and—okay, okay. Come ahead, but I'm telling you now that you're going to feel really silly...."

Lauren heaved a sigh, met Nick's steady gaze and shook her head.

"Maybe you're right. A face-to-face chat *is* in order. I'll do my best to meet your plane...what? Okay, then, take a taxi. You still have a house key? Good. Well, I'll see you when I see you, I guess. And, Diana...will you please not mention the engagement to Mother? I, um, want to tell her myself."

The moment Lauren hung up the phone she buried her face in her hands.

"You okay?" Nick asked, getting up and walking over to her chair. He dropped down on one knee in front of her.

Lauren raised her head. "Diana's flying up in two weeks to find out what's going on."

"I gathered that."

"I'm going to love looking her dead in the eye and telling her she's interfered for nothing, that this whole thing is a lie."

"You mean you're actually going to wait that long before you spill the truth about us?" He couldn't believe it.

As if already formulating just how she'd advise Diana to mind her own business, Lauren actually nodded in reply before his question really registered. Then she froze, winced and met his gaze. "Oh God. That would be awfully mean, wouldn't it?"

"I'd say so, yeah. She's your favorite sister, after all."

"Diana is my only sister."

"All the more reason not to keep her in the dark too long."

"I suppose." Lauren pulled the diamond ring off her finger. "Here, take it. There's no way out of this mess now but to tell everyone the truth, and pronto."

"Not so fast," Nick retorted, backpedaling. "While it's only right that you should tell Diana everything now, there's no way I can do the same to Phillip Avery."

Lauren arched an eyebrow in censure. "Well, if that isn't a double standard!"

"No double standard. Our situations aren't remotely similar, and there's no way I can justify this faked engagement to Avery. I mean, what am I supposed to tell the man...that I lied so his wife would get her tongue out of my ear?" He shook his head and handed back the ring. "I don't think so."

Lauren hesitated, then took it. "I hate to admit it, but you have a point." She slipped the ring back on her finger. "So we're agreed that we won't tell Avery, but do we tell Diana?"

"Absolutely."

Sucking in a deep breath as if to bolster her courage, Lauren reached for the phone and punched out a number. Almost instantly she grimaced and dropped the receiver into the cradle. "Line's busy."

"She's probably telling your mother about the engagement," Nick teased with a wicked grin.

"She'd better not be!" Lauren exclaimed, turning on him. Her eyes flashed and two spots of crimson stained her cheeks.

"Just joking, just joking," Nick hurriedly exclaimed, trying to soothe the waters he'd just troubled. "Try her again."

"I will in a minute," Lauren murmured, drawing out the sentence as if her mind were somewhere far away.

"What's wrong?" he demanded.

"Nothing really." She gave him a reassuring smile that did everything but reassure him. "What you said just served as a painful reminder of how many times Diana has irritated the holy heck out of me through the years."

Nick didn't like the sound of that. "For example?"

"For example . . . the time our Aunt Susan sent us a box of chocolates to split for Valentine's Day. Diana, who'd gotten the mail out of the box that day, hid it in her closet and didn't share for *two weeks* and only then because she'd eaten all the pieces with nuts in them."

Nick frowned, hoping he couldn't guess where this was headed.

"And then there was the time she borrowed *and broke* my favorite necklace." Lauren, sitting with her legs crossed at the knee, bobbed her foot up and down in righteous indignation. "She let me look for that thing for at least *two weeks* before she confessed."

Nick took note of the storm clouds gathering in Lauren's expressive eyes. Was her sense of honor about to get swept away in a gale of childhood memories? It sure looked like it to him. "Why don't you try calling her again? She's probably off by now."

Lauren never moved a muscle.

"Lauren . . . ?"

"I'm thinking maybe I'll let her stew awhile."

"You can't do that," Nick replied.

"Why not? Heaven knows she deserves a little grief back for all she gave me when we were kids."

"*Kids* being the key word, here. You're not a kid now, you're a grown-up. Grown-ups don't lie to their sisters."

Lauren said nothing for a moment, then gave him a guileless smile. "You know, Nick, Diana has been matchmaking like crazy ever since Lee Jacobs and I broke up about a year and a half ago."

Lee Jacobs? Who the hell was Lee Jacobs? "Er . . . sisters are like that, I guess."

"Yeah, well, she's worst than most. Always faxing me the names of eligible bachelors she knows, sending me off on blind dates whenever I visit her in Houston, lecturing me about my biological clock. She acts as if I don't have enough sense to pick out a good man by myself."

Nick's sympathy for Diana began to wane. "I'm sure that the news of our engagement didn't exactly reassure her."

"No," Lauren admitted, in the next breath qualifying that with "but only because you were such a rebel the last time she saw you."

"Right," he murmured somewhat dryly, now half-sorry he'd tried to make Lauren feel guilty for fooling dear ol' meddling Diana.

Lauren gave him a sidelong glance, almost as though measuring the state of his feelings—sure indication she played him like a piano. "She was awful to you when you guys were an item, wasn't she?"

"Not so bad," Nick murmured, to discourage her from reopening teenage wounds.

"Oh get real, Nick. She cheated on you from day one, stood you up if someone better called and wore Brent McEntyre's class ring for *two weeks* before she broke off with you."

"*Two weeks?* She had that damn ring that long?"

Lauren, eyes twinkling, nodded.

"Well, hell."

They sat in silence for a moment, each lost in thought.

"Guess I should try to call her again," Lauren finally ventured.

"What's the rush?" he retorted.

Their gazes locked. "Or I could teach her a lesson."

"Meaning?"

"We could play up our engagement for all it's worth, gain her blessing—and she *will* give us that, once she gets to know you again—then tell her the truth. That would surely prove once and for all that I do have a brain in my head and can find myself a wonderful man—"

"That *she* passed over years ago."

Lauren's smile lit up the room. "So you agree we should do it?"

Nick battled his conscience. "Diana is nobody's fool, Lauren. I'm thinking it won't be so easy to pull the wool over your sister's eyes as Sabrina's."

"True..." She thought for a moment, then flashed another brilliant smile. "Diana's not coming until the twenty-eighth...sixteen whole days—"

And nights.

"Surely if we get together a few times—"

Hmm. Impulse took rein in Nick's mind. "A few times? If we're going to fool big sis, we'd better do more than that. Now I'm going to be out of town several days the weeks she's coming in, but should be available before that." He watched Lauren's face, searching for a sign that she might go for the crazy idea now filling his head. "I suggest we spend as much time together as possible, to talk."

"Okay."

"And I think we should practice being more affectionate, too."

Lauren frowned slightly at him as if trying to read his thoughts. Nick kept his mind blank, certain his X-rated plans might be a bit much for her.

"I agree with the first part," Lauren replied, frowning slightly. "But not the practice thing. I personally think we have 'affection' nailed already, or if not *that* exactly, then a definite facsimile. Anyone watching us in the Averys' garden earlier tonight would think we've been engaged, or maybe even married, for years."

"Get real, Lauren. Anyone watching us would *know* we were kissing for the first time and had a long, long way to go before wedding bells rang."

"What are you talking about?"

"Technique. There's a world of difference between the kisses of a couple such as we, who really barely know one another, and a couple who plan to marry. Please bear in mind that I'm referring to a man and woman who don't share a roof...unless, of course, you told Diana we live together. In that case, I'll have to alter our strategy."

"You know I told her nothing of the sort."

"Good. So are we clear on this?"

"We're not clear on anything, Nick. You're going to have to explain how our kisses are different from those of an engaged man and woman."

"I'd rather demonstrate." He cocked an eyebrow at her, asking permission to proceed without words.

"O...kay." Clearly, she wasn't so sure about this.

Nodding encouragement, Nick scooted to one end of the couch and motioned for Lauren to join him, which she did with some hesitation. Just as she moved to settle herself a cushion away, he reached out and caught her arm in his hand, firmly redirecting her to sit in his lap instead.

"Now put your arms around me," he said.

Looking more amused than alarmed, Lauren obeyed by laying one arm across his shoulders and the other across his chest. He noted that she laced her fingers to hold the hug in place. In turn, he wrapped his own arms around her waist.

"Good. Now kiss me just the way you did in the garden tonight."

Eyes twinkling, Lauren leaned toward him. Nick met her halfway, opening his mouth even as she opened hers, sampling again the incredible sweetness. She sighed when he ended the kiss—sighed and released him from her hug.

"So tell me, what was wrong with that?"

"Nothing was wrong with the kiss," Nick hastily explained. "It was the rest I have a problem with."

"The rest . . . ?"

Nick nodded. "First of all, if we were engaged we'd probably be lying on this couch instead of sitting on it."

"Why is that?"

"Because we'd be hot for each other. Remember that we don't live together, so we don't have sex on a regular basis, if at all."

"Oh, yeah." She actually blushed, a reaction Nick loved.

"Ready to get horizontal?"

"Why not?"

Though Nick's conscience instantly supplied several reasons why not, he ignored them and once again tempted fate by maneuvering a change in position, all the while keeping hold of Lauren. It wasn't easy, but within moments they lay face-to-face, heart to heart, thigh to thigh on the couch.

"You're right. This is much better," Lauren murmured, her lips against his chin. "Anything else wrong with our technique?"

"Placement of our hands."

He heard her swallow, felt her heart begin to thump. "Our... hands?"

"Yes," Nick breathed, highly aware that his own heart hammered as erratically. "Mine should be *here*—" he skimmed the tip of her breast through the shiny black fabric of the dress "—or *here.*" He traced the line of her hip and thigh.

"What about my hands?" Lauren asked, the words more a gasp than a whisper. "Where do they go?"

"Anywhere you want to put them," Nick growled. "Anywhere at all."

Lauren considered the question for an eternity before she loosened his tie, pulled it over his head and tossed it to the carpet. She then unbuttoned his shirt from neck to waist.

"You're not wearing an undershirt," she said, pushing the snowy white fabric aside. "Good," she added as she raked her fingernails over the sprinkling of hair on his chest. Nick's muscles jumped in response to the teasing touch. Lauren laughed softly and did it again before asking, "Anything else wrong with our technique?"

"Hell, yes," Nick said. "We're wearing too damn many clothes."

"Then I suggest you take off that shirt," Lauren said, sassily adding, "since I've as good as done it for you."

In a flash Nick wiggled out of the shirt, not an easy task since Lauren had begun to plant kisses on his chin, jaw and neck. He groped behind her for the zipper of her dress, impatiently tugging it downward.

"Be careful," Lauren whispered when the zipper caught at her waist. Obviously attempting to help, she put one hand back, an action that shifted her body weight and upset her precarious position on the too-narrow couch.

Instantly Nick attempted a rescue. With a squeal, Lauren fell off the cushions, anyway, taking him with her. They landed with a soft "Oomph!" on the plush carpet, Nick half on top of her, their legs and arms tangled.

Lauren made no attempt to get up, instead focusing on Nick's clever hands, which still worked their magic. "I'm not sure... oh, wow... Diana will... ooh... like this."

"We're practicing... um, yeah... private technique now, Lauren. Once that's perfect, we'll... yes!... proceed to public."

Beep... beep... beep...

Nick froze. "What in blue blazes—?"

"My pager. Oh God, I forgot to answer Lisa's call! What has it been? An hour? An hour and a half?"

"Try thirty minutes," Nick dryly replied even as Lauren rolled free and scrambled on all fours to the end table—or maybe *all threes* was more appropriate since she held her dress on with one hand.

She snatched up the pager, eyed the number and groaned aloud. "It's her, all right. How embarrassing."

"She can't expect you to answer every call the moment you get it."

"Why not?" Lauren retorted. "I've done it until now." Visibly winded and not a little disconcerted, she crawled up into her chair and picked up the phone. Her gaze locked with Nick's, she took a couple of deep breaths, then punched out the number.

"Lisa? It's Lauren."

Nick watched her every move, noting how in seconds her shoulders sagged in relief.

"Diana called me here, actually. Caught me just as I was coming in the door a few minutes ago. That's, um, the reason I didn't call you back right away. I got side-tracked."

Sidetracked? Well, that was one word for what they'd been doing, Nick supposed.

Guessing Lisa had just reported that Diana called her office at some point, he heaved his own sigh of relief and got to his feet. He didn't want to put Lauren's patients—or her practice—in jeopardy. He just wanted . . . he wanted . . .

What do I want? Nick suddenly wondered. Where are we going with this?

Oh, sure, he'd claimed they needed practice in order to fool Diana, but was this the sort of activity she would ever witness? Of course not. And never mind his idiotic theory about perfecting their private technique so their public technique would be convincing.

That was hogwash and he knew it. One motive and one motive only triggered his actions tonight: need. He needed Lauren West as he'd never needed another woman. She was all that was missing from his life...excitement, laughter, easy affection, hot sex. And what was Lauren's motive for what had happened between them this night? Nick naturally wondered. Curiosity? Desire? Mutual need?

He almost laughed aloud at the thought.

The very last thing a successful, goal-oriented, level-headed woman such as Lauren West needed in her life was a man as confused as Nick Gatewood. And if he had one ounce of honor in his gypsy bones, he'd do the right thing and get the hell out, before things went any further.

"Thanks, Lisa. Sorry I took so long to get back to you." Lauren dropped the receiver back in its cradle, drawing Nick's attention to her once again. They exchanged a long look. With a teasing smile, she shook a finger at him. "You're very bad for me, Nicolas Gatewood."

"Lady, you don't know the half of it," he replied, words from the heart.

Chapter Three

Just minutes after Nick left—right after she'd hung up with Lisa—Lauren received another call, this time from one of her partners, Joelly Masters, who reported that Joelly's mother had been involved in an auto accident in Atlanta. Since she needed to leave at once to be with her, Lauren had been moved from fifth call to first. She didn't mind the change. The night was as good as over, and Saturday's call would now be fourth instead of third, hopefully resulting in fewer interruptions when she met with Nick.

For hours Lauren lay in her bed without sleeping. Her gaze was on a crystal ring holder on which hung an engagement ring she would not touch again until Diana's visit. Her thoughts were on Nick, who was such a complicated man, such a puzzle. One moment he found excuses to pull her close. The next he found others to leave and stay away. Or was his schedule really so busy they could not get together before Saturday to catch up on each other's lives? Remembering how, earlier that night, he'd hemmed and hawed as they'd struggled to find mutual free time, she had to wonder.

It was almost as if Nick had deliberately conjured up things to do on Thursday and Friday nights—an odd development considering he was the one who'd suggested they meet before Diana's visit and talk for hours. Of course, if they didn't talk any more the next time they met than they'd talked tonight, nothing would be learned anyway.

Lauren smiled at that thought, reliving every marvelous moment right up until Lisa's second page. That was when Nick had suddenly put his shirt back on, looped his tie around his neck and zipped her dress. What a shame. Why, in another few minutes they'd have—

Good grief!

Lauren sat bolt upright and tossed the covers aside. She leapt from the bed and, satin nightgown swishing around her ankles, headed barefoot down the hall and then down the stairs to the kitchen, where she raided the cookie jar of a handful of Oreos. After pouring herself a glass of milk, Lauren sat at the bar, snacking, thinking, blaming.

"Must have been the wine," Lauren decided, coming up short of any other reasonable explanation for their "serious making out" so soon after running into him again. That, combined with eighteen months' worth of celibacy and Nick's virility, had simply been too much. As for Nick, he was a red-blooded male, and who of that breed would refuse sex when it was offered to him?

So why had he ended their fun and games by suddenly getting dressed? Had the page spoiled the mood? Or had it reminded him of her warning that she could only give him leftover time? Lauren sincerely hoped it was the latter and that he'd play it smart from now on and keep his distance. Heaven knew she'd never be able to resist him if he was foolish enough to come back for more.

Poor Nick. Abandoned by his mother as a baby, raised by a rough-and-tumble fisherman who'd spent more time on a boat than at home, he'd overcome a very unconventional childhood to make something of himself. He deserved serious involvement with a traditional woman instead of a not-tonight-maybe-tomorrow love affair with a harried obstetrician.

The next two days were hectic for Lauren, who had to see her share of the missing partner's patients plus her own. Come closing time on Friday, it was all she could do to drag herself home when the clinic finally shut its doors and the weekend began. For that reason, she had already fallen into bed when the phone rang at eight-thirty. Lauren fumbled for—and dropped the receiver—before waking enough to manage coherency.

"H-hello." Her voice was thick with sleep.

"Lauren?"

"Nick?"

"Yeah. Did I wake you?" He sounded incredulous.

Lauren covered the receiver, cleared her throat, then uncovered it. "Of course not. Just had a frog in my throat." She settled back against the pillows and plucked at the comforter. "How've you been?"

"Busy. About tomorrow night—"

He's backing out! Lauren's prudent side celebrated his wise decision even as her other side—the lonely one few knew about—mourned the loss. "Yes?"

"Can we reschedule for nine o'clock? Turns out I have to meet with a client on-site at eight."

Lauren let out her pent-up breath in a slow hiss of relief. "Nine is fine."

"Then I'll see you tomorrow night at Lucci's." They'd chosen that restaurant for its size—small, its location—halfway between their houses, and its food—Italian.

"Right, oh, and Nick . . . ?"

"Hmm?"

"My call schedule has been altered slightly, so we might even get through the night without a page."

"Have I ever complained about the interruptions?"

"No," she admitted with a sigh. "But you should. You really should."

Lauren reached the restaurant minutes after nine. After a quick peek in the rearview mirror to check her hair, worn loose for a change, she slipped from the car and made her way to the entrance. The night air felt cool, rustling the silk of her dress. The high heels of her suede boots clicked on the concrete walkway. Her pager, tucked in her pocket tonight, bumped against her leg with every step.

Once inside, she discovered Nick was running late, too, so she let a hostess show her to a table for two near a window. As soon as she sat, she scanned the room, taking pleasure in the glow of the candles on each table, the sparkle of the crystal stemware, the hum of low conversations. Though the restaurant was crowded, she felt comfortably alone, confirming that Lucci's was a perfect choice for this much-needed tête-à-tête.

At that moment Nick entered the restaurant. Immediately his gaze found Lauren across the room. With a big smile at her, he waved the ever-helpful hostess aside and made his way through the tables to where she sat. Lauren could barely breathe, so bewitched was she by the sight of him. He might have stepped straight off the pages of a men's fashion magazine except that he wasn't one of the pretty-boy models so often found there. No, the man was machismo to the bone, and in a shockingly primitive way she responded to him.

"Hi, beautiful," he said as he sat, words that did nothing to shatter the spell of sexual attraction that left her dazed and breathless whenever they got together.

"Hi, yourself." Her voice was little more than a squeak, and hearing it, Lauren blushed and gave herself a mental shake. "You're late."

"Yeah, sorry. I hope you didn't wait long."

"Three minutes," she admitted, adding, "I was late, too."

He laughed, then, and, reaching across the snowy linen tablecloth, caught her hand in his. "God, it's great to see you again."

Lauren could barely contain her smile of delight at his candid confession, even though it killed her hopes that he was playing it smart.

"I've thought about you a lot the last couple of days," Nick said. "Probably because I'm still in shock at finding Sissy West all grown up and so...so...irresistible."

"Irresistible my fanny."

Nick blinked in surprise at her blunt rejoinder. "Excuse me?"

"If I'm so irresistible, how come you ran out on me Wednesday night?" If smart thinking wasn't to blame then there had to be another reason. Lauren wanted to know what it was.

He looked away instead of answering, all at once a little boy instead of the macho man who stunned her senses. Oddly enough Lauren found one as appealing as the other.

"Let's just say I had a flashback and realized I might not be up—" He grinned as if something had struck him funny. "What I mean is, I realized I might not be *ready* to get romantically involved with another woman. Things are moving awfully fast...."

"Things are moving *too* fast," Lauren said. "And I'm not at all sure that's a good thing."

"I'm glad to hear you say that, because neither am I."

"Then you agree we should just ignore this physical attraction thing and settle for friendship?"

"Friendship?" He laughed so incredulously that heads turned. "Damn, Lauren. Thanks to that little escapade on the couch, we're way past that."

"Not necessarily."

"You mean you honestly think there are times when friends undress each other?"

"Of course there are. For example, when—"

"They're sexually curious about each other?"

Lauren nodded. "Or if—"

"They were foolish enough to kiss in a moonlit garden?"

"Yes, or if—"

"The boss's wine went straight to their heads?"

With a huff of impatience, she glared at him. "It seems you have all the answers."

"All but the most important one... Where do we go from here?"

Lauren shook her head to indicate she was just as baffled as he. "Maybe after Diana leaves, the two of us can figure out the answer to that together."

"Maybe," Nick replied just as the waitress hustled up with ice water and menus. He waited until she left before adding, "And in the meantime, I suggest we try really hard to keep our relationship right where it is—somewhere between friends and lovers.''

"I totally agree," she murmured with a sigh of relief. So this wasn't going to be a problem after all. They'd play it smart. Keep level heads and cool hearts.

The next moments were spent looking over the list of entrées—a good thing since the waitress soon came back with their drinks. She took their dinner orders, then left again.

"We'd better get started on catching up, don't you think?" Nick asked. "That little pager of yours is liable to go off any minute."

"Not tonight," Lauren assured him. "I've put a hex on it."

"In that case, begin at the beginning. What happened after I dropped out of good old Texas City High?"

"Nothing much," she said. "I graduated, went to college and med school, completed a residency in OB-GYN and found a job."

"Why that particular specialization?"

"Two reasons, really. First, I figured that there were a lot of women just like me, who didn't particularly enjoy being examined by a male doc. Second, I love babies."

"Yet you don't have any of your own."

"Not yet," Lauren agreed. "I'm only thirty-two, though. There's still plenty of time to find the right kind of guy and start reproducing."

"Exactly what do you mean by 'the right kind of guy'?"

"I mean a man who has all the physical and emotional characteristics I consider a must in a mate."

"Are these essential characteristics a secret?"

Lauren shook her head.

"Then let's start with physical. What, exactly, are you looking for?"

She took her time replying, well aware that she had piqued his curiosity. "The eyes of Nick Nolte, the dimples of Tom Selleck and that dashing scar on Harrison Ford's chin. The voice of Sean Connery, the shoulders of Nicolas Cage and—"

"Enough! Enough! I get the picture." He sounded thoroughly disgusted, exactly the reaction Lauren had expected when she started teasing him. "What about his emotional characteristics?"

"The man I'm looking for is steady as a rock and very, very patient. He also has to be madly in love with me."

"You don't ask for much, do you?" Nick murmured.

"I never thought so, but would you believe I haven't found a soul to fill the bill so far?"

"You don't say...."

He sat in silence, obviously digesting her words and, judging from the pained look on his face, wishing there hadn't been so many to swallow. Lauren thought about offering him an antacid.

"Uh...ever think about lowering your standards?"

Lauren almost laughed. "As a matter of fact, I have."

"And?"

"I think I could forego the physical characteristics."

"Then if a man is steady, patient and madly in love, he'll do, no matter what he looks like?"

"Actually, he doesn't have to be *that* steady. We're all entitled to the wobbles now and then, don't you think?"

Nick gave her a solemn nod. "So all he has to be is patient and madly in love?"

"Hmm. Maybe I'd better leave patient off my list, too. I mean, I shouldn't expect him to be anything I'm not, myself."

"Are you saying that as long as the guy loves you, he's acceptable?"

"Well . . . I'd want to love him back." She rested her elbows on the table. "Now is that asking too much?"

"No." For just a second Nick stared at her, then he reached for his glass and drank it half-dry in one gulp. "Um . . . let's talk about your job."

"Where do I start?"

"With the clinic. I'd like to know why you chose that particular one to set up your practice in."

"Money was my biggest reason, I guess," she admitted with an embarrassed laugh. "I had student loans to repay and wanted to do it quickly. I liked the idea of being in practice with four other women, plus I thought I'd like the location and the exclusive clientele."

"You *thought* you would? Are you telling me it hasn't worked out that way?"

Lauren hesitated. "I have no real complaints. I mean, the building is old, but very beautiful. I have reliable co-workers and talented partners. I'm respected by my patients, all of whom pay their bills."

"But . . . ?"

"But everything is just so—impersonal." Lauren paused to let the waitress place their salads in front of them. Once they were alone, she intercepted Nick's puzzled frown. "What?"

"I'm wondering how something so intimate as a physician-patient relationship could ever be called impersonal."

"Because it is . . . at my clinic, anyway. Of necessity, every OB patient must be seen by every physician during her pregnancy, thereby ensuring that she'll have at least met the doc who's on call when she delivers."

"So?"

"So while the system works well enough, it virtually eliminates all chances to really get to know the patient."

"Why not change the system, then?" Nick asked around a bit of salad.

Lauren, herself, just pushed the lettuce around on her plate. "Because I'm the new kid on the block. Besides...no one else seems to have a problem with it." She took a bite, chewed it slowly and swallowed without tasting. "I'll never forget the time I examined a woman one month postpartum and asked who delivered her baby only to learn that it was me."

Nick winced. "Was she upset that you didn't remember the big event?"

"She was most understanding, luckily, and reminded me that her baby was the third I'd delivered in one very busy hour."

"There are worse things you can do than forget a patient, Lauren."

"I know. Yet I can't help but think about when my dad was alive and practicing medicine he carried everyone's medical history around in his head. Why, the man knew more about most of his patients than their own families knew." She pushed her salad away and gave him a half smile. "Remember how simple things used to be? You got sick, you phoned the doc, he fixed you up. Now we've got call schedules, answering services, co-pays and deductibles, not to mention persistent pharmaceutical salesmen with so-called free samples. It wears me out."

"Poor Lauren," murmured Nick.

"Oh God, I've been whining, haven't I?" She felt her cheeks flame. "I'm sorry, and I'm changing the subject. It's your turn to talk."

"Not so fast," Nick said just as the waitress returned to take their salad plates. He waited until she set their entrées on the table and left, then spoke again. "As your intended, I believe I'm entitled to the juicy details of each and every past love affair."

"Get real. My life before our 'engagement' is my business and mine alone."

"Aren't you forgetting that Diana and I once dated?" His eyes twinkled with mischief . . . or was that just a reflection of the candle's glow?

"So?"

"So she knows I'm the jealous type, and, therefore, naturally interested in my fiancée's romantic history."

"You're the jealous type?" She feigned shock and took the bread basket he passed to her. "We could tell her you've changed."

"Just how much change do you think big sis is going to buy? I've already metamorphosed from rebel-without-a-cause into architect."

"Hmm. You do have a point." Lauren heaved a lusty sigh, grateful for the lighter mood. "What, exactly, do you want to know?"

"For starters . . . how many times you slept with that Lee guy."

"Nick!"

"All right, okay. I'll rephrase that. How long were you two an item?"

"Two years."

"*Two years?* And you never married?"

"We had a lot of problems, and, fortunately, the good sense to doubt that we'd last if we ever tied the knot."

"So what happened?"

"Six months after I went into full partnership at the clinic, Lee split. He said he couldn't handle my busy schedule. I think he was also a little jealous of my salary."

"Ah, the age-old battle of the sexes." He took a bite of his lasagna, which must have tasted heavenly if his look of utter appreciation was anything to go by.

"Exactly," Lauren replied, before digging in to her own.

"And the guy before Lee?"

"How'd you know about him?"

Nick grinned. "You just told me."

Rats! So she had. "Marty was a physical therapist I met while I was in med school."

"And how long did this relationship last?"

"Three years, off and on."

Nick shook his head as if unable to believe she could date a man for so long. "Who left who this time?"

"I did the honors."

"The problem?"

"Marty needed a maid and a hooker, not a medical student who had better things to do than stroke his fragile ego."

"I...see."

"Good, because I've said all I intend to say on the subject of past loves. It's time to talk about you, Nicolas Gatewood. Time to—oh, hell." Lauren drew her vibrating pager from her pocket, glaring at Nick when he grinned.

"Am I saved by the, um, page?"

Lauren read the number of her answering service. "I'll let you know in a minute. Don't move." That said, she left the table and found a courtesy telephone. Her shoulders sagged when the operator gave her the home number of the partner on third call.

"Great," Lauren muttered, instantly assuming there must be some sort of scheduling crisis. This particular partner was getting bad about swapping call on short notice, thanks to the romantic impulses of her globe-trotting boyfriend, a movie director she met while acting as technical consultant for a film. Lauren, who hadn't much of a social life, usually didn't mind. Tonight, however, she did.

As expected, the boyfriend was in town and demanding attention. Promising herself that this was the last time she'd be talked into extra work, Lauren made her way back to the table, where Nick had just finished up his lasagna.

"Here," she said, sitting down and scooting her plate in his direction. "Eat mine, too. I have to go to the hospital and back up the partner on second call."

"Shouldn't the partner on third call be doing that?"

Oddly pleased that Nick apparently understood what was really a very complicated schedule, Lauren had to smile. "Yes, but her *beau* has flown into town unexpectedly and has plans."

"And what about *your* beau's plans?"

"If you were really my beau, I'd tell her tough luck."

"But I'm not."

"No, you're not."

"So I *am* saved by the pager."

"Only for the moment. Get out your calendar, Nick, and I'll get mine out, too. We'll schedule our next meeting right now."

"I'm free whenever you are."

"Since when?" Lauren asked, peering at him over the top of her open appointment book.

"Since we decided to remain in the never-never land between friendship and sex."

Insulted, if not surprised, that he'd lied about his busy schedule, Lauren laid her book on the table and met his gaze square on. "Were you that afraid I'd complicate your life?"

"No," he said. "I was that afraid I'd complicate yours, and from what I can see, it's complicated enough already. So when's it going to be?"

"Tuesday? I'll most likely be on third call."

"Tuesday, it is. Where?"

"Let's make it my place. I'll grill hamburgers or something."

"Great. What time?" Nick queried.

"Seven?"

"I'll see you then."

Lauren left him seated alone at the table for two, eating her lasagna.

Sunday afternoon Nick jogged in the park to work off all the pasta he'd consumed the night before. After the run, he sat on a bench to people watch, something he found himself doing more and more on weekends, maybe because so many families came to the area.

Nick saw moms, dads and their tykes on picnics, cycling and skating. He watched in amazement as a sleek Labrador retriever caught a Frisbee. He rescued a little girl's kitten from her brother's remote-controlled race car.

In short, he tried the role of family man on for size—a part he could never really hope to play. Not that he wasn't a skilled actor. He was, as proved by the fact that he lived where he lived, worked where he worked, dressed as he dressed and drove what he drove. Friends and co-workers thought of him as successful and happy. No one—most of all not Lauren—guessed that deep inside, a rebel in black leather revved up his motorcycle and seethed to be set free.

Lauren...sweet, sweet Lauren. She was the reason he now found himself on this park bench, longing for what he could not have. For all her preoccupation with schedules and her dedication to duty, she was a woman who could make him wish his childhood had been normal, wish he'd learned the skills necessary to ensure a happily ever after, wish he were capable of lifetime commitment.

Did she have any idea what kind of man he really was? Nick had to wonder. Of course not. A woman such as Lauren—classy, conventional, caring—had better sense than to get involved with the renegade likes of him. Her desire was based on appearances which were nothing more than a lie his continued silence perpetrated. And knowing she would leave if she learned the sad truth, he wasn't sure he had the guts to confess.

Monday passed without incident for Nick, beyond some curious stares of a couple of co-workers. He wondered if Phillip Avery might've talked when he shouldn't have, sharing the news of his so-called engagement. Since no one congratulated him, however, he chalked the glances up to the retirement rumors still flying around. That night he talked to Lauren on the telephone long enough to find out what he could contribute to their meal the following night.

Tuesday flew by, a day filled with difficult decisions, last-minute changes and unexpected projects. Somehow Nick managed to finish everything that came his way and in time to leave his office by six. He drove to Lauren's by way of his favorite supermarket, stopping there to pick up potato chips and cola.

He rang Lauren's doorbell without hesitation this time, then, when she didn't answer, walked to the side of the house to see if her car was in the garage. It wasn't, so Nick settled himself on the porch swing to wait.

Thirty minutes passed, then an hour, during which the clouds overhead sprinkled rain and the lights came on in the neighboring houses. Finally Lauren wheeled her late-model hardtop into the drive. She was out of the car in a flash, clearly upset.

"Oh, Nick, I'm so glad you waited!" she exclaimed as she dashed up the steps. "We had one crisis after another—"

"That's okay."

"—and Joelly Masters is still in Atlanta—"

"It's okay, Lauren."

"—and then I had to stop at the meat market."

Nick caught her shoulders in his hands and as good as yelled. *"Yo. Lauren!"*

"What?" she demanded, wide-eyed with shock.

"You don't have to apologize."

"Actually, I'm not. I'm simply explaining why I'm late."

"Do you think you could do it while we cook? I'm starved."

"Great idea." She tried to turn away, a movement Nick prevented by laying a great big kiss right on her lips. She sighed and melted in his arms, all softness and femininity, yet capable of bringing him to his knees.

To his knees? Heavens, yes, though flat on his back would be better as long as she was over him. The thought of *that* raised his pulse to triple digits and affected a certain susceptible part of his anatomy. Grateful for the shadows of evening, Nick set Lauren away from him.

"Wow! What was that?" she asked, visibly shaken.

"A Gatewood hello," Nick replied, taking her groceries and her keys. "And if you think that was something, just wait until you get a load of the goodbye."

Shaking her head, Lauren pointed out the right key. Nick used it to unlock the door, then motioned her inside and followed, carrying both his plastic grocery bags and hers.

They both prepared dinner. While Nick took care of grilling the burgers, Lauren toasted the buns, threw together a salad and set out the dinnerware. Finally they sat together in her kitchen, Nick on one side of the glass-topped table, Lauren at his left. They talked little—Nick having cleverly resisted her one attempt to question him about his past. There'd be time enough for that later, he thought.

Once they finished eating, Nick sent Lauren off to shower and change while he cleared the table. He whistled while he worked, enjoying the tasks that were such a bore at home, but fun in someone else's kitchen. Lauren, freshly scrubbed and looking not a day over twenty without her makeup, soon joined him there, and together they walked into her den and settled themselves on each end of her couch.

"So talk," she ordered, turning sideways on the couch so she could face him. When she started to tuck her feet up under her, Nick nixed the move by setting them in his lap. He then began to massage the soles. "If you're trying to distract me," Lauren said, with a heartfelt sigh, "it's working. Oh God, it's working."

"Now why would I do a thing like that?" he teased.

"Because you don't want to talk about yourself?"

Nick grimaced. "Obviously you know me well."

"Are you kidding? Your life is a mystery, which is the reason you're here. Tell me everything that's happened since you dropped out of high school."

"Well . . . you know about the army."

"Six countries in seven years, right?"

He nodded. "And you know about the G.E.D. and the college degree."

"Yes, and *you* know how very proud I am of the man that you've become."

She would say that, he thought, feeling a pang of guilt undoubtedly left over from Sunday's visit to the park. "So what is it, exactly, that you want me to talk about tonight?"

"I want to know more about the woman you wouldn't commit to—the one who threw that beautiful ring at you," Lauren answered much to his dismay. "I believe if I were your fiancée I'd know about that. I also want to know about your childhood."

"I'm surprised you haven't heard that sordid tale already," Nick replied, picking the easy topic first. "Small towns are good for that."

"Mmm-hmm." To Nick's surprise, Lauren lifted her feet up, swung them to the floor and scooted closer. Turning her back to him, she asked, "Would you work the knot out of my shoulder, there? It's been killing me all day."

Dutifully, Nick began to knead the muscle in question, his thoughts on the past. "I'm sure you know my mother ran away from home when I was two."

"Yes, and I know that you were raised by your dad. What I don't know is if you ever heard from her again."

"Several times, from several different states. Once she even came to visit us—brought some guy with her, not the guy she left Texas City with, but another one. I remember that she always seemed so restless and dissatisfied with whoever and whatever she had at the time. My dad, on the other hand, lived in the same house in the same city and fished off the same boat his whole life." Nick laughed without humor. "It was damned lucky for me that he did, of course, but I'm so much like my mom that I don't see how."

"What are you talking about?" Lauren murmured, maneuvering herself so that Nick could reach the other shoulder, too. "You're not a bit like your mom."

Nick, who'd automatically begun to minister to the other shoulder, tensed at her words, knowing they were the perfect lead-in to the confession weighing so heavily on his mind. "Actually, I'm just like her—undependable, uncommitted, always searching yet never knowing what for."

"That's not true."

"It is true." Abruptly, he slipped his arms around Lauren's waist and tugged her back against him so he could rest his chin on the top of her head. Relishing the closeness that was surely about to end, he sighed. "If there's anything you need to know about me, anything at all, it's this—I'm a man who breaks engagements, Lauren. I'm a man who breaks hearts."

Chapter Four

Taking Nick's hands in hers and loosening his embrace, Lauren turned so that their knees touched.

"First, if that woman had been the right one for you, you'd never have hesitated to marry her. Second, while there are lots of adjectives I could use to describe you, *uncommitted* is simply not one of them. What about your education? You started and finished college, didn't you? That took commitment. As for *undependable*, well, you're the first person I'm going to yell for if I get in a tight spot because I know you'll be there for me. You're that kind of guy."

Struck momentarily silent by her foolish, blind trust, Nick had no reply.

"Don't be so hard on yourself," Lauren continued. "You're only human, after all, and entitled to make a few mistakes. No one is immune. Why, I've even made one or two, myself." At that she grinned, considerably lightening the moment, not to mention Nick's heart.

He knew he should argue, maybe do a better job explaining. *Later,* he promised himself and, with a slow grin, reached out to pull her into his arms again. Taking advantage of the fact that they were face-to-face this time, Nick kissed Lauren tenderly, putting into the caress all the emotions for which there were no words. She seemed to understand his unspoken language. At any rate she sighed and snuggled closer, then raised her face to be kissed again.

As had happened the last time they'd engaged in light lovemaking on that couch, Nick soon found reason and means of stretching out, except this time he lay on his back, Lauren full on top of him.

"I thought we decided not to do this sort of thing," she murmured between kisses planted on his chin and cheek.

"This is as far as we'll go," he breathed, and then proceeded to kiss her deeply, all the while exploring with his hands every feminine curve within reach. When her clothes prevented some of the intimacies he craved, he simply unbuttoned and unzipped.

Lauren cooperated in every way, somehow managing a little unbuttoning and unzipping of her own. Her touch seared his flesh. Her kisses drove him wild. Suddenly near loss of control, Nick grasped Lauren's shoulders and sat her up. While this put distance between their upper bodies, it only worsened the contact below the waist, since she now sat astride him.

"Is something wrong?" she asked, her voice seductively husky.

Nick let his gaze sweep her tousled hair and flushed cheeks before dropping it to her breasts, encased in a lacy pink bra, and then her flat belly, tantalizingly visible through the open fly of her jeans. She was fantasy come to life. And hell, yeah, something was wrong—for her, at least. Never mind that he'd warned her what kind of man he was. She wasn't listening. If he had any scruples...any scruples at all...he'd do the noble thing and stop this before they went too far.

"I can't . . . I can't . . . ."

"Yes?" Lauren softly prompted, then wetted her kiss-swollen lips with the tip of her tongue.

Nick groaned aloud. "I can't undo this." He slipped his finger into the valley between her breasts and tugged on the fastener of her bra.

"Oh." Lauren reached for the plastic hook, which she released with a simple twist. At once the elastic band pulled the cups apart, baring her flesh to his hungry eyes. "Better?"

Nick didn't bother to reply. With a soft sigh of defeat, he reached for Lauren, who pressed into his touch and further fueled the fire raging inside him.

They kissed deeply. He pulled her down on him again, relishing the way her curves flattened against his bare chest. *Heaven* had she called this? Well, she had that right, and to hell with good intentions.

Beep . . . beep . . . beep . . .

"No," he groaned, tightening his hold on her.

"Yes," she replied, her voice shaky with regret.

Mentally cursing the gods who tempted his patience—or were they just looking after Lauren?—Nick allowed her to slip off him and step over to the phone. He barely heard her one-sided conversation, so entranced was he by the sight of her standing half-dressed and not a bit self-conscious . . . just out of reach.

"All right. I'll be there in fifteen."

The receiver clinked into its cradle. Lauren shifted her gaze to Nick. Her expression said it all.

Abruptly he sat up. With a smile of regret, she joined him on the couch again, this time perching on the edge of a cushion.

"Poor Nick."

"Does that mean you're not disappointed?"

"No..."

Lauren's voice cracked, and she looked away, but not before Nick saw that her eyes shimmered with what could be tears. Surprised, he caught her chin in his fingers and made her look him in the eye again.

"What's this?" he asked just as a teardrop fell from her lashes and snaked its way down her cheek. Solicitously he brushed it away.

"Fatigue. Frustration." She paused as if fresh out of words. "My life is simply not my own these days, and while I knew it would be this way, somehow I expected more... reward."

"You mean money?"

"I mean personal satisfaction... the feeling that I've made a difference in someone's life, that I've done something worthwhile that no one else could, or would, do."

"Maybe what you need is a vacation."

"It's going to take more than that, Nick," she replied, getting to her feet and automatically refastening, rezipping, and rebuttoning. "Much, much more."

Nick did the same, letting her assist when his trembling fingers refused to do the task with any degree of efficiency. When she finished, she slipped her arms around his waist in a brief hug from which Nick did not immediately release her.

"Do we dare to schedule another meeting?" he asked.

"I'm game if you are."

"Good. What call are you on tomorrow night?"

"Fourth."

"Thought so. Why don't we meet at the amusement park at six? The change of scenery will do us both good. We can talk while we navigate the tunnel of *luv*."

"Sounds like fun," she replied, stepping back so she could tuck her blouse into her jeans. "But isn't the park a bit public?"

"That's exactly why I suggested it," Nick admitted, and then waited for her reaction to his belated attempt to prevent certain heartache. One more night on the couch would surely be the end of their friendship and the beginning of a love affair he believed would not turn out well for either of them.

She tried to hide her disappointment by smiling, but her eyes gave her away.

"I'm honestly trying to save you, Lauren."

"From what? You?" Lauren laughed and scooped up her purse and car keys. Moving toward the door, she added, "I'm a big girl, Nick. I can take care of myself. If anyone needs saving, it's you—from this never-stopping merry-go-round I jokingly call my life."

"That's exhaustion talking," Nick commented as he followed her to the door. "Not the Lauren I know and lo—" Just in time he caught himself. Sticking that shocking *L* word back to analyze later, Nick amended his statement. "Not the Lauren I know."

"You're right," Lauren agreed, apparently not noticing his near slip of the tongue. "And after a good night's sleep, I'll be fine."

"Wish I could say the same." Swiftly he kissed her, a noisy contact that made her laugh and put the twinkle back in her eye. Braving the rain shower in progress, Nick soon loped across the lush wet lawn to his car.

"Tomorrow," he promised before sitting behind the steering wheel and slamming the door.

She waved in reply and, ducking against the rain, ran to her own car. As always they went their separate ways, but suddenly lonely at the sight of the taillights disappearing around a corner, Nick had to wonder if she hadn't taken part of his heart with her this time.

It was almost midnight that night, before Nick finally extracted from a corner of his mind the *L* word he'd stuffed there earlier. Lightning streaked across the sky. Thunder rolled, and hard rain pounded the wooden deck and splashed up on his bare feet and legs. Seated on a lawn chair under the protection of the eave, Nick sipped a glass of orange juice and barely noticed the storm.

Instead he puzzled over how close he'd come to telling Lauren he loved her, when he really didn't. Not that there weren't strong feelings between them. There were—mutual desire being number one. Before he explored that particular feeling any further, he wanted to be certain she understood his limitations. Although a dedicated lover, he made a poor fiancé. And while a loyal companion, he was not husband material.

How nice it would be to see her again tomorrow night, Nick nonetheless realized. Not only would he have a reason to get out of bed in the morning—assuming he ever crawled in it tonight—he'd have something to look forward to all day, too.

Nick frowned at that and suddenly wondered when work had become so boring that it took a date with Lauren to brighten up his day. Thinking back, he realized that for months now he had dreaded going to the office. Projects that had once challenged him were now a drag.

It looked as if that old white-line fever, that recurring ailment for which there seemed to be no cure, had caught up with him again. Thanks to it, he'd never been able to stick with anything besides the army, which had provided so many travel opportunities, for more than four years.

He thought of the jobs he'd held down, the women he'd held close. Too many. Even pursuit of his education had involved three different colleges and a couple of changes in major. It didn't bode well for a future at Avery, Sanders and Wright, Nick realized. As for a partnership in the firm...he doubted himself capable of the commitment such a career move would entail.

"I need some good advice," Nick said aloud, and then instantly thought of Lauren. Who better to advise him than Dr. West, a pro at commitment to profession, who needed, more than anyone else, to hear what he had to say? He would talk to her tomorrow, he promised himself, even as a glance at his watch revealed tomorrow was now today. Groaning his exhaustion, Nick promptly headed indoors to his bed—big enough for two, but wasted every night on one.

"Did Mrs. Crawford pick up her insurance papers?" Lauren asked as she slipped out of her lab coat and hung it on a peg near the door to her office.

"Her chauffeur did," replied Lisa, her red-haired, hazel-eyed secretary. Seated in one of the antique chairs in Lauren's tastefully furnished office, she referred to a notebook she held.

"Good. Did Mrs. Maxwell schedule her mammogram?" Lauren sat in her leather executive chair, pulled a couple of hair clips out of the desk drawer, then grabbed a brush out of her purse and began to furiously use it.

"Her social secretary made it for next Wednesday at two." Lisa watched in visible fascination as Lauren tried to pin back her thick mane with only the aid of a tiny hand mirror she'd propped on the desk.

"Okay. Now what about Karen Lange? Did you call to give her the results of her lab work?"

"I left word with her answering service that we had the information," Lisa replied, adding, "Let me do that," as she tossed aside her book and rose to step around the corner of the desk. In seconds she unpinned what hair Lauren had pinned and redid it. "You must have a hot date tonight."

"It's not 'hot.' In fact, it's not really even a date. I'm just meeting a . . . um . . . *friend* to discuss some things."

"The guy who called last week? Nick Something-Or-Other?"

"Mmm-hmm."

"Is he as handsome as he sounds?" Lisa asked.

"Every bit as."

"Are you in love with him?"

Not a bit offended by the nineteen-year-old's curiosity—dating was the girl's life, after all, not to mention a rarity for Dr. West—Lauren smiled. "I just told you he's a friend. A good friend I like an awful lot."

Lisa worked some tendrils of auburn hair free of its pins to form a wispier frame for Lauren's oval face. "When do I get to meet him?"

"Probably never." Lauren eyed the results in her hand mirror, then caught sight of Lisa's disappointed face just over her shoulder. She set down the mirror and turned to face her young secretary. "We're just working on a project together. When it's finished, we'll undoubtedly go our separate ways."

"But why?" Lisa demanded. "I mean, he sounded so nice and all, and you've been so happy since you started dating him. Couldn't you two just hang out for a while or something?"

"I suppose we could," Lauren answered. In truth, she knew better. Hanging out sometimes led to hanging on, and she was too attached to Nick already.

Lauren reached the amusement park at the moment Nick did, so she parked her car beside his. Together they walked to the entrance, where Nick paid for their admission.

"Food first," he said, taking Lauren's hand and leading her to a nearby concession stand. Minutes later they found a tiny table and sat down knee-to-knee to feast on pizza slices, curly fries and funnel cake.

Every bite was nectar to Lauren, who had skipped lunch. The moment she finished and dabbed her napkin to her lips, Nick scooped up their trash, tossed it in a nearby Dumpster and sat back down. "While we let this digest for a minute, I want to ask your opinion about something."

"Okay," Lauren answered with a shrug. As inconspicuously as possible, she inhaled the spicy scent of his cologne. It wasn't difficult to do since he had propped his elbows on the tiny table and leaned very close.

"Do I look like the kind of guy who could be a partner at Avery, Sanders and Wright?"

Lauren caught her breath. *"Did they offer you the job?"*

"No."

"But you're still thinking about it?"

"Worrying is more what I'm doing, actually."

"Why on earth?" she asked, vaguely recalling her previous impression that Nick wasn't wild about the idea of partnership and curious about it. "I mean, you love what you do, don't you?"

"Yes, of course. Well, most of the time. Lately I'm not sure." Nick heaved a sigh. "It's not the work, Lauren, it's the job."

"I can relate to that," she murmured somewhat dryly, "since I know for a fact that sometimes when we get what we want, we don't want it anymore. So tell me, why did you take the position you have now?"

"Money," Nick said without hesitation. "The almighty buck has influenced all my career moves, in fact. And now that I finally have enough of it, I'm starting to second-guess my choices."

"Again, I can relate. So what are you going to do if they ask you to join management?"

"I was hoping you'd have an idea or two."

Lauren bubbled with laughter. "I can't believe you'd come to me for advice after my whining about my job every time we get together."

"You don't whine."

"I do, and I'll tell you why. Mind if we take a walk?"

Nick shook his head. He got to his feet, waited while Lauren got to hers, then took her hand, leading her down the paved midway. They strolled in silence for a moment, absorbing the sights, smells and sounds that were an amusement park. Then Nick nudged her with his elbow. "So why do you whine?"

"Because just like you I regret my career choices. I'm making no contribution to the world, you know, something my father did on a daily basis in Texas City. People needed him. He mattered. And while he wasn't wealthy by most men's standards, he was rich in respect and love.''

"Sounds as if you need to move to a small town."

Lauren considered that option and murmured, "Maybe," before she stopped short in front of the Ferris wheel, a move that nearly tripped Nick. "Want to ride?"

He looked high overhead at the topmost seat, turned a little green and shook his head. "I prefer flat to the ground and fast, thank you."

"Oh, come on."

With a groan Nick let her drag him to the ticket booth. Minutes later they slipped into one of the seats and secured the safety bar. Almost at once, the big wheel turned, raising them up over the park.

"Now this isn't so bad, is it?"

Nick just shook his head. Eyes ever on the inky night sky instead of the ground, he scooted closer and laid an arm across her shoulders. "Tell me about your clinic. All I know is that you have the craziest call schedule in the world and an interesting secretary named Lisa."

"She is one of a kind, isn't she?"

Nick nodded.

"I have a better idea than just talking about my clinic. Why don't we drive over there, instead? For that matter, why don't we drive to your office, too? Now would be the perfect time, when no one is there to see us together and ask questions."

"Great idea," he said, instantly signaling the man running the Ferris wheel to stop it so they could get off. Luckily no one else was on the ride, though Lauren doubted that would have mattered to Nick.

* * *

They drove to Nick's office first, by way of Lauren's house, where they left her car. Located in a building which looked as if it had been sculpted from glass and steel, the offices were ultramodern and tasteful, if a bit sterile. Lauren noted that there were no family photos on the desk—not a big surprise—or anything else personal and felt a stab of sympathy. For all her petty squabbles with Diana and her frustration with her headstrong mother, who lived in a retirement village in Florida, Lauren could not imagine life without them.

After a brief tour, the two of them drove to Lauren's clinic, several miles away in an older neighborhood. Nick commented on the classic architecture of the building. Lauren responded by giving him a guided tour of the waiting room, lab and exam rooms, pointing out each and every thing she would change if she were in charge.

Nick offered many suggestions for modernization, but seemed to run out of words when they reached the very last exam room in Lauren's wing of the building.

"A penny for your thoughts," she said, fully expecting—and actually looking forward to—a lengthy list of renovations that would transform this cluttered area into a spacious, efficient exam room.

To her surprise Nick flushed beet red. "I'm not sure they're worth that."

"Try me."

"Er, I was just wondering what you'd say if I told you to take off your clothes and lie on the table."

With a huff of exasperation, Lauren threw her hands up and, spinning on her heel, exited the room. Nick followed. Once in the hall, he grabbed her arm, turned her back around to face him, and gave her a decidedly sheepish grin.

"Sorry about that."

"You're sorry all right," Lauren retorted, finally giving in to the laughter nearly choking her. She added a playful punch to his gut before asking, "Where to now?"

"I was thinking my place for coffee. It's just a couple of miles from here."

"Coffee sounds wonderful." Lauren led the way back to the waiting area. When she would have moved on to the exit, Nick stopped her and pointed to a bulletin board, mounted on the south wall. Clearly he hadn't noticed it when they came in.

"What's that?" he asked.

"Our brag board." She stepped over to it, taking him with her. "It was my idea. An attempt, I guess, to get closer to my patients by displaying the baby photos so often sent to us. Aren't they precious?"

"I don't know," Nick murmured, peering at one photo in particular. "This little guy looks remarkably like a prune."

"He does not!" she exclaimed. "He's beautiful, and his parents are very proud of him, just as I would be if he were mine."

At once aware of Nick's thoughtful stare, Lauren realized her envy must be showing. Acutely embarrassed, she forced a smile to lighten the moment, then quickly hustled him out of the office.

A half hour later found Nick in his kitchen, measuring coffee grounds and water. Once the wonderful aroma of the brew filled the kitchen, he walked back into his den, where Lauren stood at a wall of shelves, perusing his reading material.

Nick winced, knowing what she would find there: Westerns, science fiction, tattered hot rod magazines and back issues of *Architectural Digest*. Not particularly heavy stuff, he realized, seeing things through her eyes.

He walked over to his answering machine, which indicated he'd received one call, and pushed the playback button. After a whirring noise that indicated the tape was rewinding, the voice of his secretary could be heard.

"Nick, this is Marilynn. I'm calling to tell you that Mr. Avery phoned just seconds after you left work today to invite you to a Halloween party on Saturday, the twenty-ninth, at Christopher Sanders's house. It's mandatory that you attend, probably because they're finally going to make the big announcement, and you have to wear a costume—"

Nick groaned.

"—so you'd better reserve one ASAP. I'd do it for you, but I'm off the rest of this week and next week, too...remember?"

He heard a definite smirk in her voice and wondered at it. She was usually more sympathetic to his social woes.

"Good luck, and I'll see you in twelve days. Oh, and Nick—"

Her voice really dripped with sarcasm now.

"Mr. A. said to please bring your lovely fiancée because everyone is dying to meet her."

So that was it. Avery had blabbed, and now Marilynn thought he'd gotten himself engaged without telling her.

"Damn!" Nick exclaimed, instantly intercepting Lauren's look of dismay. Reaching out, he cut off the answering machine and plopped down on his corduroy couch.

"You know that Diana will be in town on the twenty-ninth," she said.

At once he brightened. "So she will. Guess we'll have to send Mr. A. our regrets."

Lauren abandoned the bookshelf to join him on the couch. "But your bosses are going to make their big announcement."

"That's just a guess."

"You still have to go—and without me."

Nick shook his head and sank deeper into the couch, legs stretched out in front of him. "You heard Marilynn, my secretary, I'm supposed to bring you with me to satisfy everyone's curiosity. Since she didn't know about the engagement, I'm guessing that 'everyone' really means the other two partners."

"In other words, this engagement of ours may better your chances of joining management."

"Maybe, and you know I'm not sure that's what I want."

"Your uncertainty is reason enough to play along for a while. Who knows how you'll feel about things tomorrow?"

Nick winced at the truth of that. Maybe she had him pegged, after all.

"Surely Diana can entertain herself for a few hours on Saturday night so I can go with you to the party."

"You mean you'd leave her alone after flying up just to see you?"

Lauren laughed without humor. "Just to see me? Ha! She's coming up to check *you* out, bud, and it will serve her right if she has to sit home alone on a Saturday night while the two of us party. In fact, this might even make our engagement appear more realistic.''

Nick dropped his head back and stared at the ceiling, all energy long gone. ''Isn't it amazing how one little lie has complicated our lives?''

''Yes,'' she agreed. ''And I'm wondering now how we'll ever undo it.''

''It'll be embarrassing for all concerned. In fact, at this point, it might really be easier to do it than undo it.''

Lauren gaped at him. ''You mean get engaged?''

He nodded.

''I can't believe you'd say such a thing, even in jest.''

Nick raised his head and locked his gaze with hers. It was time to find out if she really had received the message he'd been sending. ''Why not?''

''Because marriage to you is out of the question.''

''Why?'' he repeated, oddly hurt even though that was the answer he wanted. He straightened his body so that he sat upright on the couch. Casually, he rested his ankle on the opposite knee.

''Because life with a doctor—male or female—is hell, and you, of all people, deserve better than that.''

Though tempted to demand an explanation for her unexpected, undecipherable comment, Nick hesitated. She looked as if her thoughts were miles . . . or maybe it was years . . . away. He almost hated to intrude.

Almost. ''What's on your mind?''

Lauren blinked, then gave him a half smile. ''I'm thinking about a tea party I once held in my backyard. I must have been four or five years old. My guests were Raggedy Ann, Winnie the Pooh and Barbie.''

Nick chuckled at the picture her words painted.

''At that point in time, all I wanted to do was grow up, get married and have lots of babies.'' She brushed nonexistent lint off her pants, a self-conscious gesture to Nick's way of thinking. "Somehow those childhood dreams were replaced by an adult desire to make it in a man's world. Now there's no turning back, even though what I got isn't exactly what I always wanted."

Reaching out, Nick directed her gaze to his. "What would make you happy?"

She shrugged. "Maybe moving to a smaller town, like you mentioned before. I have a cousin who's a pediatrician and works in Arkansas. She loves what she does and seems to find plenty of time for her husband and twins."

"So what's stopping you from packing up and moving on?"

"You," Lauren answered, her voice now light and teasing. "You did just propose, remember? Are you willing to give up your job here in Dallas and move, too?"

"Actually, the idea of starting completely over somewhere in rural America does hold a certain amount of appeal."

"You're really serious, aren't you?" Lauren's eyes were round as cupcakes, confirmation she hadn't been listening when he tried to confess his restlessness and inability to commit.

"Yes. You're not the only one who'd like to make some kind of contribution during your lifetime. It's not as easy for an architect as it is a doctor, though."

"Since when did you run from a challenge?"

"Since I proposed to you," Nick teased, taking his cue from Lauren. "Are you ready to give up your highprofile job and run away?"

"I am if you are," she retorted, words surely spoken in jest. But for once her eyes did not sparkle with mischief, and when she finally dragged her gaze away long moments later, Nick was disconcerted to find himself wondering just how serious she was. "Do you suppose the coffee is ready yet?"

"Damn," Nick muttered, leaping to his feet and hurrying to the kitchen. He poured the long-forgotten coffee into mugs and carried them, steaming, back to the den. He noted that Lauren had found the remote control and turned on the television, a sure indication she didn't want to talk anymore.

That was okay with him. They'd talked enough this night—too much, in fact. As a result, his head now swam with foolish notions and farfetched dreams he knew would torment him for days, maybe weeks, to come.

Chapter Five

There were no hugs or kisses that night, which did not surprise Lauren. All the crazy talk of marriage seemed to have put a damper on their moods, and no wonder. Mismatches such as they had no business engaging in such foolish, conjectural conversation.

Lauren heard not a word from Nick on Thursday or Friday. And though she hadn't really expected to—they knew more than enough about each other to fool big sis—she couldn't help but be disappointed. Nick was that much a part of her life now. In fact, the focus of her existence had shifted so completely that twenty-four hours without the sight or sound of him equaled a totally forgettable day.

Dangerous territory, this area between friendship and love, she realized. Once there, it was hard to tell where one stood, not to mention which way one was headed. As for a way out of the place... there wasn't an exit in sight.

On Saturday, Lauren slept late, then drove to a café a couple of miles from her house. Seconds after she sat down at a table intended for four, her pager began to vibrate. Lauren grumbled until she displayed the caller information, then brightened when she recognized a number she'd memorized but never used: Nick's.

In a heartbeat, she stood at the pay phone. He answered on the first ring.

"Nick? It's Lauren. What's up?"

"You, I hope. I waited as long as I could before calling in hopes I wouldn't wake you, then got your answering machine, so I paged you. Only after I did that did it occur to me you might have the machine taking your calls so you could sleep until noon."

"Not me. I'm actually at the Willow Street Bistro, waiting on the waitress to take my breakfast order."

"I know the place. Are you alone?"

"Yes."

"Any plans beyond breakfast?"

"No."

"Then write my name down on that handy-dandy appointment book of yours and stall the waitress until I get there."

"Do you want me to block out one hour or two?"

"I'll need all day," Nick said, somewhat cockily adding, "And you might pencil me in for all night, too."

"Don't you wish?" she retorted, light-headed at the thought. Smiling all the while, Lauren then hung up the phone and did as requested.

Not half an hour after, Nick strolled into the café. He greeted her with a quick kiss on the lips, then sat at her elbow. At once the waitress appeared at their table with thick porcelain mugs and a pot of hot coffee. Without so much as a glance at the menu, Nick ordered pecan waffles, the house specialty, a request Lauren echoed. Then, the moment they were alone once more, he leaned close and kissed her again, longer this time. "We should've made love Wednesday night."

Lauren nearly choked. "What brought that on?"

"Two whole days without you," Nick said. "I've been lonely."

"Well, Mr. Lonely, unless you're keeping secrets there's no way we could've made love Wednesday night. You have to be *in* it to *make* it, you know."

"Good point. I stand corrected," he replied. "As for my keeping secrets... I've been nothing but honest with you."

And never once mentioned love. "I know," Lauren murmured, even as her heart took a sudden, unexplainable plunge into despair.

At that moment the waitress brought them plates piled high. When she left, Lauren made sure the topic of conversation changed.

"So do you have specific plans for today?"

"Yes, *we* do," Nick told her around a bite of his breakfast. "We're going to find and reserve costumes for that party next Saturday. I have a whole list of places to try, thanks to Phillip Avery's secretary. I want you to go along so we'll match."

"Hmm. Any particular theme in mind?"

"Nah."

"Then how about Antony and Cleopatra?"

This time it was Nick who nearly choked. "Can you really picture me in a toga?"

Lauren couldn't. "So we'll go as Robin Hood and Maid Marian, instead."

"No lime green tights for me. Any more bright ideas?"

"Just one—a biker and his chick."

Nick tensed, his cheeks flaming crimson, a reaction that surprised Lauren, who only meant to tease.

"Did I say something wrong?" she instantly demanded.

"No," he replied after a moment's hesitation. "It's just that the folks at Avery, Sanders and Wright don't know about the Harley in my garage."

"Neither did I, actually, but I'm not surprised." She didn't speak for a moment, instead wondering just how much of himself he had suppressed to play this role of clean-cut architect. It was almost as if the glimpses she'd had of the *old* Nick were really glimpses of a *secret* Nick. No wonder he grew restless with his life. Who wouldn't? "Do you really think it would make a difference to them?"

"Knowing how conservative Misters Avery, Sanders and Wright are, I never had the nerve to chance it." He gave her a questioning look. "Does the bike make a difference to you?"

"Of course not. I've ridden on it, remember?"

"Yeah. Want to ride on it again?" Though his tone was teasing, Lauren sensed a certain seriousness that told her she was being put to some kind of test.

At once it was critical that she pass it. "Why, I'd love to."

He positively beamed his pleasure. And basking in the warmth of his smile, Lauren realized just how much more there was to the man than he had revealed so far. Instantly excitement shimmied up her spine, and adrenaline pumped through her veins.

With a start she realized she hadn't felt so stimulated in years. Could it be that every day she, too, played a role that wasn't right for her?

* * *

They spent the next half hour fueling the motorcycle, donning appropriate clothing and helmets and packing a picnic lunch. Lauren tucked her cellular phone in with the peanut-butter sandwiches in hopes she could prevent a sudden end to the impulsive outing. With luck, today's third call would produce no crises she couldn't handle over the telephone.

By one o'clock, Lauren sat astride Nick's gleaming black Harley-Davidson, her front pressed against his broad back, her arms around his waist. The wind plucked at her clothing and whistled around the helmet he'd dug up from somewhere, but she didn't care. It was glorious speeding down the highway—a race to freedom, to fun.

Nick, who seemed to know every back road in the area, soon left the traffic of Dallas far behind. They didn't slow until they reached a narrow dirt road, down which he turned the bike. A half mile later, he braked to a complete halt and pointed to a pond.

"How's this for our picnic?"

Lauren took a good look at the pond, partially shaded by a massive oak tree, and heaved a sigh of pure pleasure. "Perfect."

Nick reached back to help her off the bike, then dismounted. Together, they gathered up the satchel that held the picnic things and a thermos. They then walked up a grassy incline to the edge of the water.

Since breakfast hadn't been so long ago, they didn't eat right away. Instead they sat on the lush grass to talk. Lauren felt as if she'd left the real world far behind and now dwelt in some fairyland where call schedules did not exist. She guessed Nick felt the same. At any rate, when he stretched out and reached for her, the look in his eye said he wasn't thinking of his office or any old costume party.

She went to him without hesitation, lying half on top of him, their bodies molded from shoulder to toe. In seconds their lips touched, too, and her heart began to pound with forbidden sexual thrill.

"Will you make love with me?" Nick asked.

"Make love, or have sex?"

Nick hesitated, his face a study in bemusement. "I have to admit that I honestly don't know. Does it make a difference?"

"Yes. If it's love you want to make, then I'll have to pass because my life is complicated enough. On the other hand, if you want simple, no-strings sex, I might consider it."

He blinked, clearly surprised by her answer. "Are you sure? I mean, I thought we already talked about this and decided to stay cool."

"That's what I thought, too."

"Yet you just said yes."

"Only because you just asked."

Silence reigned for maybe half a minute, during which Nick's thoughtful gaze never left her face. "If we did make lo—I mean, have sex—would it be just a one-time shot, or could we, um, do it again?"

"As far as I'm concerned, we could do it as many times as our busy schedules permit, providing of course, that we're careful. I'm not on the pill, and though modern enough to have an affair with you, I still cling to at least one traditional value, namely marriage before babies."

Nick tensed, then spat out a four-letter word that shocked her.

"What?" she demanded, rolling aside so he could bolt upright.

"I don't have any."

"Traditional values?"

"Protection, Lauren. Protection."

"You mean you don't have a stash in your wallet?"

"No, dammit. Do you?"

"No."

They shared a look of dismay before the irony of their situation hit home. At once, Lauren bubbled with laughter. "It's probably a good thing, you know. All this sunshine and fresh air has surely addled our wits. Why else would we be sitting here talking so casually about sleeping together, a life-altering decision neither of us has given a moment's thought?"

"Speak for yourself, Lauren," he grumbled.

"You mean you've thought about it?"

"Every minute of every day since we met at Texas Stadium."

"Yet you aren't prepared."

He shook his head. "I never dreamed you'd go for it."

"Why not? I've all but tackled you to the ground every time we meet."

"And here I thought I tackled you."

They stared at each other without speaking for a moment. Lauren could feel the tension in Nick's body, knew that he was still sexually excited and as ready for her as she was for him.

Goose bumps danced down her arms. Her heart thumped like a tom-tom. "Didn't we pass a service station right before we turned off the pavement?"

Nick drew a shuddering breath. "That was a church."

"Oh." Lauren closed her eyes to block out the sight of his face, beaded with sweat, and was instantly treated to a Technicolor daydream of the two of them mouth-to-mouth, skin-to-skin, *one*. She gulped, knowing a solitary word could set the wheels of an affair in motion. Did she dare take the risks? Did she . . . ?

"Maybe we could—"

"No."

Lauren frowned. "But you don't even know what I was going to say."

"Sure I do, and the answer is still no." As though sensing her keen disappointment that he'd turn her down, Nick gave her a kiss, then got to his feet. "That was the most gracious gift anyone has ever given to me, and I want you to know that I'll never forget it."

"But I didn't give you anything yet," Lauren protested, scrambling to her feet, too, and standing toe-to-toe with him.

"You gave me your trust," Nick said. "You told me that you believed I was capable of being a daddy and a husband."

"But you *are*—"

"I'm not." They exchanged a long look, then Nick picked up a rock and, as if suddenly self-conscious, tossed it into the woods to the east. "I'm feeling really restless. Want to go for a walk or something?"

"Since we've just eliminated 'or something,'" she said with a sigh of frustration, "I guess we'd better walk."

They did walk, talking about everything but sex—a subject too volatile for safe handling. Lauren noticed that the exercise did wonders for Nick, who was able to joke and laugh again by the time they ate a late lunch. She felt out of sorts, herself—disappointed, relieved, confused.

At three Lauren's pager beeped, announcing a minor problem she handled successfully via phone. At three-thirty, it beeped again, a bigger problem that necessitated they return to Dallas. Nick drove Lauren to his house, where she'd left her car. Before she slipped behind the steering wheel, they shared a long kiss, during which she felt him tense with desire.

Regretfully she stepped away from him, ending it. "Will I see you before Friday?"

"Probably not. I'm flying to Jackson Hole, Wyoming, on Tuesday and won't be back in Dallas until Friday around noon."

"What's in Jackson Hole?" Lauren asked, belatedly remembering his warning that he'd be out of town the week before Diana's arrival.

"Not what, who. An old army buddy of mine, William Many Horses." He tucked the tips of his fingers in his jeans and rocked back on the heels of his boots. "He bought some land in the mountains a few months back. I promised I'd fly up and draw the blueprints for his cabin."

"You must be one heck of an architect for him to by-pass the locals and call you."

Nick grinned. "I work cheap."

Lauren, who suspected *cheap* really meant *free,* grinned back. "I envy you your vacation. Have fun and call if you miss me." She started to slip behind the steering wheel, only to pause when Nick caught her arm.

"There's no *if* to it, Lauren," he said, his tone suddenly serious. "I'll miss you."

"It's about time you got home!" Diana exclaimed when Lauren finally dragged herself through her front door at seven-fifteen Friday night after a very hectic week at the clinic. Though all four of Lauren's partners were on the job and fully functional, she had still seen five patients more than she considered enough for one day.

"Sorry I'm late," Lauren replied, reaching out to hug her big sister.

They had gone through all stages of sisterhood, the two of them, from being inseparable to barely tolerating each other. At this point in time, they were close, if not best friends.

When Diana stepped back, Lauren noted that she wore an apron. At once she sniffed the air and sighed with pleasure—spaghetti. There were certainly merits to having the food editor of Houston's largest newspaper for a sister.

"I was going to take you out for dinner," Lauren said.

"And make me miss a chance to whip up something in that gorgeous kitchen of yours?" Diana retorted with a toss of ash blond hair. "No way. Now why don't you have yourself a hot shower then come to the kitchen so we can talk before Nick gets here." She sounded more like hostess than guest.

"Nick's coming over?" Contrary to his prediction that he'd miss her, he obviously had not. At any rate, he hadn't called even once during his four-day absence.

"Seven-thirty," Diana replied from halfway down the hall. A second later she disappeared around the corner.

Instead of heading upstairs to freshen up, Lauren followed her to the kitchen. "You've talked to him, then?"

"Yes, about an hour ago. He called expecting to find you home. Told me he'd just flown in from Wyoming. Something he said made me think that his plane was delayed . . . ?"

Lauren nodded, thankful Nick had mentioned arrival time when telling her about the trip. "He was supposed to be in at noon."

"Oh. Well, it's a wonder we didn't run into each other at the airport, isn't it?"

"Yes," Lauren murmured, backing out of the kitchen before Diana could ask questions about Nick's trip—about which Lauren knew next to nothing—or the engagement ring she wasn't yet wearing.

Her mind on Nick's imminent arrival, Lauren dashed upstairs and showered in record time. She applied a minimum of makeup, slipped on jeans, a sweatshirt and the engagement ring, then headed out her bedroom door. Halfway to the stairs, the front doorbell rang.

"I'll get it," Lauren yelled toward the kitchen, hoping for a few seconds alone with Nick before they assumed their roles.

"Oh, no you won't," Diana retorted from the foot of the stairs. Before Lauren could protest, she threw the front door open wide. "Hello, Ni— *Oh my God.*"

Lauren, by now halfway down the steps, stopped short at Diana's exclamation of shock. What's wrong? she instantly wondered, watching anxiously as Diana tugged Nick into the house. He looked fine to Lauren—more than fine, in fact—dressed in a polo-style shirt, khaki pants and leather deck shoes. Respectability personified.

"Where's the black leather?" Diana demanded, eyes twinkling, a question that reminded Lauren of her own reunion with Nick. She hurried down the stairs to rescue the man, who looked a bit flustered.

"Hidden deep in his closet," Lauren interjected, stepping between her "fiancé" and her beautiful sister. She actually felt a twinge of what could only be jealousy and marveled at the oddly familiar feeling. Was Diana, then, right in her claim that Lauren had a crush on Nick all those years ago? Impossible...or maybe not. "Hi, babe. Did you have a good visit with, um—" *What on earth was Nick's friend's name?* "—Charlie Many Houses?"

Nick never missed a beat. "Yeah," he replied, reaching out, engulfing her in a warm hug. He then kissed her—a rather chaste kiss no doubt calculated to convince Diana that their engagement resulted from a levelheaded decision, not passionate impulse. Nonetheless that kiss kick started Lauren's heart. "Mmm," he breathed right in her ear, a sound obviously for her benefit only. "I missed that."

That? And what about *me?* Lauren silently demanded, hurt that it was apparently their physical encounters he'd missed instead of their mental ones. In a flash she realized she should expect nothing more. In another, she wondered about Wyoming—where he'd gone, what he'd done and who with.

"I'm glad you're back," she said, forcing herself to smile. "And I'm glad Diana volunteered for KP. It'll be a lot easier for you two to get to know each other again here instead of some restaurant."

"Exactly what I thought," Diana said. "You guys come with me to the kitchen. Everything's just about ready."

Taking Lauren's hand in his, Nick trailed Diana down the hall so slowly that Lauren ran up on his heels. The moment big sister stepped into the kitchen and out of sight, Nick whirled and caught Lauren up in his arms. He kissed her again—hungrily, deeply—his hands everywhere at once.

Flustered, more than a little irritated, Lauren pushed him away and brushed past to enter the kitchen. Nick followed a second later, his expression so guarded it was unreadable.

"Now you sit there, Lauren." Diana indicated a seat to her left. "Nick, I want you across from me so we can talk." She motioned them to sit, then turned to the stove to get the spaghetti.

At once Nick's gaze nailed Lauren to her chair. She shifted her own gaze to Diana. "Want me to help with that? I mean, this is my kitchen and you are my guest."

"I'm your sister, not your guest. And the only thing I need help with is locating the Parmesan cheese."

"I have a box of the grated kind in the pantry. I'll get it." Lauren started to rise, only to sit again when Diana waved away her assistance.

"I'm already up." In a heartbeat she vanished into the walk-in pantry, leaving Lauren to wonder at her uncharacteristic graciousness.

She was still wondering when Nick instantly demanded, "What gives?" in a loud whisper.

"Shh!"

"We have fifteen, maybe twenty seconds alone here, Lauren, so no games. Tell me why you're angry, and *tell me now.*"

"I couldn't possibly in that amount of time."

"Then you can forget the fiancé thing. I'm a lousy actor on a good day, and so far this one has been the pits."

Fine, Lauren wanted to reply, but when her mind leapt ahead to consider consequences, the word stuck in her throat. "You didn't call, not even once, while you were away."

Nick's jaw dropped. "I was *camping* with Will Many Horses."

Oh God. She'd gotten the name wrong.

"Here it is." Diana appeared from nowhere to set the familiar green Parmesan cheese container on the table. Removing her apron, she slipped into a chair and reached for the salad bowl. "Help yourself. I cook but I don't wait tables."

"You don't clean the kitchen, either, as I recall," Lauren said, watching Diana place a helping of salad directly onto her dinner plate. Long ago their mother had taught them to eliminate extraneous plates and flatware. Unfortunately the conservation didn't extend to pots and pans, at least when Diana cooked. "I'll probably be in here washing up until midnight."

Studiously keeping her gaze averted from Nick, she selected a garlic roll from the bread basket, then scooted the basket toward him. She next scooped spaghetti, which Diana had already mixed with the sauce, onto her plate, then took a bite.

"Well worth cleanup duty," Lauren announced, trying to get some sort of conversation going. The tension between her and Nick was almost a palpable thing.

"Thanks." Diana passed the spaghetti to Nick and the salad to Lauren, clearly oblivious of any undercurrents between the two of them. "So tell me about your trip to Wyoming. Business or pleasure?"

"A little of both. I have an old army buddy, who lives near Jackson Hole. He promised me a camping trip if I'd come look at his land and then design a house that won't intrude on the landscape."

Diana giggled. "So Mr. Many Houses needs another one?"

Lauren winced at the awful joke, which was her fault and hers alone. Raising her gaze briefly to Nick's, she gave him a half smile of apology for getting his friend's name wrong. Nick ignored her.

"It's really pretty out West, isn't it?" Diana said.

"Beautiful," Nick agreed. "Especially the wilderness that my friend owns. He's so far away from civilization that he doesn't have access to running water, electricity *or a telephone line.*"

"In this day and age?" Laughing her disbelief, Diana glanced at Lauren. "I'd survive about ten minutes."

"Me, too," Lauren murmured, well aware that Nick explained all this for her benefit and wishing her behavior hadn't necessitated it.

"He doesn't have a road, either, but promised to build one since it will be difficult, if not impossible, to get lumber in there otherwise."

"Hmm." Diana's blue eyes flashed with curiosity. "Sounds as though you love what you do," she commented, beginning a question-and-answer session that lasted through dinner, dessert and a move to the den.

Nick endured the inquisition with remarkable aplomb, answering each and every question and asking a few of his own. Lauren, a silent witness, learned more about him during that three-hour visit than she had in all the others . . . no real surprise. They'd never talked as much as they should have, each time distracted by each other's physical attributes. Tonight was definitely different, thanks to Diana's presence. Aside from that one slipup just before dinner, Nick kept his hands and lips to himself and emotional distance from Lauren.

Not that he was so obvious about it that Diana noticed. He wasn't, and, as far as Lauren could tell, Diana didn't.

Seated next to Lauren on the couch, Nick kept one arm draped across her shoulders and constantly included her in his conversation with a smile or a playful tug on her hair. All the same, Lauren felt a definite chill in the air, and knew she had only herself to blame.

At last Diana yawned and then stood, signaling an end to the third degree. "All at once I'm just wiped out. Hope you two don't mind if I head for bed. No, don't get up..." She waved Nick back in his seat, gave him a smile and began to walk away from the couch, pausing at the door of the den to say, "It seems you've done quite well for yourself. I'm glad Lauren found you again."

"So I pass inspection?" Nick asked.

"Let's just say that preliminary results are promising," Diana replied in arrogant, big-sister fashion.

Lauren could not resist a sarcastic retort. "I'm sure Nick and I will sleep better tonight knowing that."

"As if you two will sleep at all!"

"Excuse me?"

"Oh, come on. I may be an old married lady with two kids, but that doesn't mean I don't remember what it's like to be crazy in love and back together after nearly a week apart."

Crazy in love? At once big sister's meaning hit home. Lauren nearly choked. Springing from the couch, she joined Diana at the door and then as good as dragged her into the foyer. "I can't believe you said that."

"And I can't believe you're trying to pretend that Nick doesn't know the way to your bedroom." Diana hooted with laughter, no doubt in response to the look on Lauren's face. "Relax. I'm your sister, not your mother. And speaking of Mom, I promise I won't tell her that you and Nick have already practiced the honeymoon. She's as old-fashioned as ever."

"Mom? *Our* mom? Nah!" Lauren exclaimed with not a little sarcasm. Their mother was so behind the times that she wouldn't even call her seventy-five-year-old boyfriend on the telephone for fear her friends would think she was a loose woman.

"I also promise not to come out of my room tonight. You two can be as rowdy as you want."

"Diana!"

"Lau-ren." The words were a taunting singsong that set Lauren's teeth on edge.

"But you don't understand—"

"Hey, I may not have graduated from medical school, but I know the facts of life. I really and truly do."

Chapter Six

Lauren's steps dragged as she walked back into the den. One glance at Nick told her he'd heard every word and thought the whole situation rather funny.

Suddenly out of sorts, she strode right on past the couch, through the dining room, straight to the kitchen, where the dirty dishes waited. She didn't turn around, but knew Nick followed and wasn't surprised when he began to clear the kitchen table.

"You don't have to help," Lauren told him as she shifted the spaghetti pan from the countertop range to the sink. Turning back to the island, she sprayed down the finish of the smooth-top range with a foam cleanser and wiped it spotless with a wet cloth.

"I think I do."

"Why? Diana will never know. *She's* promised to stay in the guest room the rest of the night so we can get as 'rowdy' as we want." Finished with that task, Lauren turned back to the sink and began to rinse out the dishes there.

Nick ignored her sarcasm as if he knew it stemmed from her frustration and embarrassment. "My helping has nothing to do with your sister. I ate, therefore I wash up. I've been a bachelor too long to think the good fairy comes in at night and does the dirty work." He handed her a stack of plates. "Besides...we need to talk. I want to know why you were so upset when I got here, and don't tell me it's because I didn't call you from Wyoming. I'll never believe it."

"You'd better." Lauren set the plates on the counter and turned to Nick, her sudden, intense remorse surely evident on her face. "Because that's the reason, and I'm so sorry. Who'd have thought I'd ever get in such a snit because you didn't hike a hundred miles across the mountains to call every night? I don't know what's the matter with me. I can only assume that my hectic workweek has so scrambled my brains that I forgot this whole engagement thing is fake."

"No apology necessary," Nick murmured, leaning against the kitchen counter, his body close. "You aren't the only one with scrambled brains. Not only did I just grope you in the hall as if I owned your body, would you believe that hiking out of the mountains to call you this week did cross my mind...and on more than one occasion?"

"Really?" Lauren struggled to hide her smile of surprised pleasure.

Nick nodded. "Will gave me hell over it, too."

"You told your friend about me?"

"We talked about lots of things...." He seemed to be hedging, which piqued her curiosity.

"What, exactly, did you tell him?"

"That I'd run into the sister of a former girlfriend just over three weeks ago, and that my life was now hopelessly tangled with hers."

"That's an awful way to put it," Lauren grumbled, shifting her attention back to the sink. Automatically she resumed rinsing off dishes so she could load them in the dishwasher.

"You're right." Nick never moved from his spot at her elbow. "*Hopefully* tangled would be a lot nicer—"

"If not as accurate." She tucked a glass plate in the rack and picked up another.

"Oh, I don't know about that. I'm finding myself increasingly hopeful as the days roll by."

"Hopeful this stupid engagement will hurry and die a natural death?"

"Actually, I think I'm hopeful it won't."

The plate slipped from Lauren's hands. Though she and Nick both made a grab, it hit the floor and shattered.

"Don't move," Nick ordered, eyeing with some alarm Lauren's dainty, ballerina-type house slippers now surrounded by shards of glass. Scooping Lauren up into his arms, he stepped over to the cooking island and set her directly on the range.

She squealed more from reflex than fear. The surface was stone cold, after all, and clean, too. Laughing, Nick put his arms around Lauren's waist and pressed against her. She parted her legs, allowing him to get even closer, then crossed her ankles behind his thighs to keep him there before slipping her arms around his neck. For a second they just stared at each other, their faces so close she could not get his features into focus. Then his mouth covered hers.

Fevered, wild, Nick's kiss quickened Lauren's heart rate, tingled her toes and tightened her gut. She caught her breath, overcome and overheated as surely as if the burners of the stove on which she sat had been red hot.

Nick, clearly reading her response as encouragement, kissed her cheeks, her chin, her nose, her eyes. His lower body moved seductively against hers, hinting at pleasures that could be hers for the asking.

"Diana thinks...we're going...to have sex...tonight," he murmured between kisses.

Lauren frowned. Weren't they well on their way to doing that already?

Nick kissed away her frown. "I'm sorry we have to disappoint her."

They had to disappoint her? Lauren couldn't imagine why.

"Sissy? Nick? Did I hear something break?" It was Diana, and sounding too close for comfort.

"Broom!" Nick demanded, his voice a frustrated whisper.

Mutely Lauren pointed toward the nearby utility room. After releasing her so abruptly she nearly toppled off the island, Nick vanished through the door. Just as Diana stepped into the kitchen, he stepped back out— broom in one hand, dustpan in the other. Lauren noticed he kept the pan in front of him, just about button-fly high.

"Hold it!" he called to Diana. "Are you barefoot?"

"Yes."

"Then you'd be wise to stay where you are. Lauren's dropped a plate. There's glass everywhere."

Taking her cue from Nick, who somehow managed to sound cool as a flimflam man with a victim in his sights,

Lauren gave her sister a sheepish nod of agreement. "Slipped right out of my hand."

"Thank goodness it wasn't the china Granny Carter left you," Diana murmured.

She watched Nick sweep, apparently oblivious to the way he kept his back to her, though Lauren wasn't. Every bit as sexually primed, Lauren noted how gingerly Nick moved and wished she could assist in solving his problem.

Diana's gaze shifted from Nick to the dishes in the sink, few of which had been loaded into the washer. "Is there some burning need to clean up the kitchen tonight? You two are making me feel guilty."

There was a burning need, all right, but it had nothing to do with the dishes—or common sense.

"How else will I ever train Nick right?" Lauren asked.

"Good point and good luck," Diana murmured, leaving them with a sleepy smile and a wave.

Neither Nick nor Lauren moved another muscle until they heard the door of the guest room shut. Then their gazes locked.

"What now?" Nick asked, setting the broom aside and walking back to the island.

"Anything besides what we were doing," Lauren replied. Laughing somewhat shakily, she added, "This engagement of ours isn't a license to make out, you know."

"Nor is it a reason to have sex."

"Oh, I don't think we can blame our near misses on the engagement."

Nick grinned and lifted her from the stove. "No, we can blame those on your pager, my stupidity and your sister. I credit the engagement with keeping us together . . . or do you think we'd have conjured up another excuse?''

"Time will tell, I guess." She inspected the floor, which appeared free of glass, then got back to work at the sink.

Nick followed. "Meaning?"

"Meaning once Diana's back in Houston we'll find out. Meanwhile, I wouldn't mind a teeny-tiny hint as to your plans. I believe you said something about being *hopeful.* . . ."

Nick nodded. "I was trying to tell you that I'm not sure I can let you vanish from my life now that I've found you again."

Lauren breathed a sigh of relief. "I'm so glad to hear you say that. I feel exactly the same way."

"Then I guess what we need to figure out is what category I'm going to fall into when I'm no longer your fiancé. I believe the choices are acquaintance, friend, lover or—"

"We're way past the acquaintance stage, Nick."

"I think so, too."

"As for friend, I—I'm still not sure it's too late for that."

Nick's short, humorless laugh told Lauren that *he* still was. "For the sake of discussion, let's say it is. That leaves lover and—" he hesitated as though searching for a word "—beyond."

"Yes."

"Is lover a viable option in your life?"

Lauren gravely considered the question, her heart rate accelerating with every passing second. Was the role of lover one that she could, in good conscience, let Nick play?

"I think lover is the only option since marriage is out of the question," she murmured. "Without legal ties to bind him, any companion who found my schedule too much could just up and leave at any time...no harm done."

"And those babies you want?"

"Later, Nick. Later."

"How much later?"

"Oh, one year, two years, five."

"Is it safe to have a baby that far past thirty?"

"Yes, and why all this sudden interest in childbirth? Are you suggesting that the category beyond friends— the only other one into which you might fall—is really *husband?*"

Nick started to speak, then clamped his mouth shut and just shook his head.

"Then I suggest we eliminate that fourth category— and all this go-nowhere baby talk—and get back to the third...lover."

"But is it wise to waste time with a lover when you should be scouring the city for your Mr. Right?"

"It is if that lover is you—a man I'd really like to have in my life."

"I'm a black sheep, Lauren. You're a lamb."

"Oh, for—!" She took a deep breath to calm her temper. "I've been on my best behavior since I met you, okay? What you've seen so far is not necessarily what you'd get if we were honestly involved. I'm bossy, grumpy, finicky, unreasonable and impatient. More important, I—"

"—surely do know what to say to turn me on," Nick finished for Lauren, suddenly pulling her close.

She caught her breath. Imperfection turned him on? Mmm . . . yes. Apparently it did. Lauren raised her gaze to Nick's and waited for a hot kiss that never came.

"You need to think hard on this."

She had to laugh at his unfortunate terminology. "With *hard* on my mind how can I think rationally at all?"

Nick groaned. Releasing her, he stepped back. "We'll talk about this again after Diana leaves."

"You're damn right we will."

They exchanged a look, then Nick nodded and abruptly resumed rinsing dishes. Feeling a little dazed, Lauren helped . . . until her pager began to vibrate and the real world intruded once again.

The midnight moon shone full and bright, casting a silver glow. Nick's Harley shot down a stretch of lonely highway that narrowed in the distance to a vanishing point, neatly halved by a broken white line. He ducked his head against the wind and, hands gripping the handlebars, lost himself to the powerful roar of the engine.

It was a race to nowhere, with neither opponent nor pursuer, yet he rode as if his very life were in jeopardy.

And maybe it was . . . at least life as he knew it. Change was imminent. There was no denying that. Tomorrow night he would learn what was going to happen at work. Sunday afternoon he would learn what was going to happen with Lauren. Of the two, his future with her mattered most.

Odd, that. Nick could remember a time when nothing was as important as his career. Now . . . *now* . . . the challenge of finding time with Lauren mattered more and consumed his thoughts.

Did that mean he was committed? Not by a long shot. Experience had long since proved that enthusiasm for a new thing didn't mean anything. Hadn't he also been excited about the army, college, his other fiancée? He had. Yet invariably he'd tired of them and moved on. Then there was the matter of his work, which had become so boring that a job offer from Will Many Horses—one that involved not only a move out West, but a cut in prestige and salary—had actually tempted him.

Lauren is different...

The thought was as fleeting as a whisper on the wind, but it left its mark on him. Yes, Lauren was different. So different that he might not tire of her as quickly as he tired of everyone and everything else. In fact, if he grew tired of anything it would be sharing her with her partners and patients.

And Lauren? Would *she* grow tired of *him?* Nick laughed aloud, a sound the wind snatched away. Hell yes, she would grow tired of him...the moment she realized just how miserable her life could be when linked to that of a restless rebel who was never satisfied, never really happy, and who simply moved on when the going got tough.

Sure he'd tried to explain how things were, how *he* was. But had she listened? Believed? Thinking on it, Nick came to realize that she couldn't have. If she had, the possibility of their becoming lovers would never have been discussed in the first place.

Clearly another talk—another explanation—was in order. He would mince no words this time. He would lay it all out on the line. He'd make sure she understood what lay ahead. He'd verify that she didn't care. And if, by some miracle, being lovers was still an option with

Lauren, then, by God, he'd go for it and never look back . . . not even when he left her somewhere down the road.

You're a fool—

Yeah, a fool. Loving and leaving invariably hurt—*him* more than the lucky woman left behind.

"What's your pleasure?" Lauren stood by the open refrigerator, eyeing her sister, who had just walked into the kitchen and who, at least in Nick's opinion, looked a little green around the gills. "Nick brought donuts—" she pointed to a box on the breakfast bar near the stool on which Nick had just sat "—or I could scramble up some eggs?"

Diana groaned and put a hand to her belly. "Oh God, no. Just a 7UP and a couple of saltines, please."

Lauren frowned at what sounded to Nick like a damned odd request for nine o'clock on a Saturday morning. "Are you sick?"

"Pregnant. Two months."

Lauren caught her breath, then emitted a yell that surely woke her neighbors. Slinging the refrigerator door to, she rushed to her sister and engulfed her in a bear hug. "Why didn't you tell me before now?"

"Payback for your not telling me about the engagement," Diana retorted with a so-there nod. Then her expression softened. "That and the fact I only found out last week and wanted to tell you to your face."

Nick wasn't surprised when Lauren's gaze found his. She looked guilt stricken. He felt the same. Lying to family and friends was not particularly fun. He wished he'd never started the charade, but if he hadn't, where would he and Lauren be now?

Living separate lives, he suspected. Exactly what they would be doing after their talk. And just when was that much-needed talk going to take place? Later, he silently promised. After Diana left, but before he and Lauren did anything she would regret.

"Oh, Nick, isn't this wonderful news?" Lauren exclaimed, turning to walk over to the bar and throw her arms around him.

Feeling for the moment as if he were a part of not only her joy, but her family, Nick could only sigh with regret for what could never really be as he hugged her back.

"Congratulations," Nick said to Diana. He resisted releasing Lauren for just a second—long enough for her to give him a questioning look—then reluctantly let her go. "This will make how many?"

"Three." Diana rolled her eyes. "I must be crazy."

"What you are is a wonderful mom," Lauren said, pulling out a chair, motioning Diana to sit in it. She then collected saltines from a decorated tin and the canned drink from the refrigerator.

"Show Nick those last pictures I sent you of the boys," Diana said around a bite of cracker.

Stepping back to the refrigerator, Lauren took several three-by-four photographs from the door, where they'd been suspended by decorative magnets. Though Nick had noticed the photos were there, he hadn't looked closely at them, so he did now.

"Cute kids," he told Diana, more appreciative of the way Lauren rested her chin on his shoulder so she could look, too, than of the children, towheaded boys who looked to be somewhere between the ages of four and six. Nick was no judge of such. "Twins?"

"Yes."

"A handful?"

"Two handfuls." Diana shook a finger at him. "And you may as well wipe that grin off your face, Nick Gatewood. In case Lauren hasn't mentioned it, she's planned on having four of her own ever since she was a kid, herself. You guys will have to get busy if you're going to get them all hatched before she hits the big four-oh."

"This is an assignment I accept with great enthusiasm," Nick murmured, feeling a total heel.

Lauren did nothing but avoid Nick's gaze, a sure sign she felt the same.

Decidedly pink of cheek now, a color that Nick thought looked better on her than green, Diana looked from one to the other of them. "When is this wedding, by the way? Please say soon. I'd rather not waddle down the aisle to be your matron of honor."

"Who said you were going to be in my wedding?" Lauren demanded, neatly sidestepping the first question.

"No one, but I let you be in mine, didn't I?"

"Does this mean we have your blessing, then?" Another question answered with a question. Nick silently applauded Lauren's skill.

"Of course." Diana beamed at them both. "I think you two are absolutely perfect for each other, and I'm sorry I ever thought you weren't."

Instantly Lauren's gaze found Nick's again. He could almost read her unasked questions: Do I tell her the truth now, as planned?

Nick shook his head just enough to tell her he had no answers. If anyone should know how to handle a mother-to-be, it was Dr. West. And besides, the woman was her sister.

Lauren took a deep breath. "About the wedding..."

So she was going to do it. Silently Nick gave her full marks for courage.

"Oh, let me get my calendar first," Diana said, leaping up to rush from the room.

Lauren threw her hands up in utter exasperation and turned to Nick, who simply did not know what to say, so kept his mouth shut. In a flash Diana was back with one of those thick leather appointment books some women couldn't function without. Nick, himself, relied on his secretary to remind him of everything.

"Okay," Diana said as she sat back down and opened the book. "This is October, almost November. If you have the wedding sometime before the first of March, I should be okay...."

"Diana, I—"

"Mother would love it if you chose February. In fact, when I told her about the engagement, she said she hoped you'd pick Valentine's Day since that's when she and Dad got married."

"You told Mother about the engagement?" Lauren, white as the snow on Will Many Horses's mountain, sank down on a chair as if her knees had suddenly given way, which, Nick suspected, they had.

"Why, yes...." Diana glanced from one to the other of them.

"But I asked you not to." Lauren's eyes flashed with temper. Her cheeks flamed scarlet. Nick winced, glad he wasn't in big sis's shoes.

"You asked too late, okay? I called her the minute Frank told me."

"Why on earth didn't you say so?"

"I don't know. I guess I was just so ticked..." Her voiced trailed to silence.

Nick thought she looked ready to cry, and not wishing to witness what could be a really sloppy scene, eased off the bar stool and toward the door.

"I'll tell you what," Diana said. "You can tell Mom about the baby."

"I don't want—stay right where you are Nicolas Gatewood!—to tell Mother about the baby. That's your right, just as it was mine to tell her about the engagement."

Nick froze midstep, marveling that Lauren had known he was escaping even though she'd never so much as glanced his way.

"I'm sorry, Lauren. What else can I say?" A big tear rolled down Diana's cheek and splashed onto the table.

At once Lauren sagged with defeat. "No, I'm the one who's sorry. Really. I know you did it in innocence. I don't blame you. I just...just...well, never mind. It doesn't matter." It was with visible difficulty that she was so gracious, and Nick's heart went out to her.

"Are you sure?"

Lauren glanced toward Nick, who managed to give her a smile of encouragement. "Yes."

Diana sniffed and looked back at her calendar, which she quietly closed. "About the date for the wedding. Anytime is okay. I don't really mind waddling."

For the second time in as many minutes, Lauren took a deep breath. "Actually we haven't set a date, but I'll, um, let you know, okay?"

"Okay."

So she wasn't going to tell her sister the truth. Well, Nick couldn't blame her since he would never have been able to do it himself. Shaking his head, he walked back to his bar stool and sat down once more.

"I guess family etiquette demands that I offer you an apology, too," Diana said to him.

Nick grinned and shook his head. "Don't waste your breath. I was raised by a dad whose idea of good manners was laughing when he belched his beer. I don't have the first clue about etiquette, family or any other kind."

"Your upbringing was rather nontraditional, wasn't it?" She shook her head as if recalling stories he'd shared with her the few weeks they'd been a pair. "And you're now marrying a doctor, which means your marriage won't be conventional, either. Poor Nick, or should I say lucky Lauren." Diana smiled affectionately at her younger sister. "At least he won't have any preconceived notions about what comprises a perfect wife."

"Good, because he's certainly not going to get one." With a smile that obviously took effort, Lauren stood. "Did I mention that Nick and I have to go to a party tonight at his office? It's a mandatory thing. Halloween-ish with costumes."

Diana bubbled with laughter. "Who are you going as—John Dillinger and his Lady in Red?"

"Why, that's a great idea!" Lauren exclaimed, turning to Nick. "What do you think?"

Treated to a vision of Lauren in a slinky red dress, Nick nodded his agreement. "You've got a dress?"

"Have I *ever* got a dress," she replied with a sassy wink.

"Surely you're not going to wear the one with the neck cut down to here—" Diana placed a finger halfway between her heart and her belly button "—and the slit cut up to here—" now she touched her hip.

"It might be too much, now that I think about it," Lauren said.

"Wear it," Nick interjected. He wanted to see that dress. "And I'll go find myself some pinstripes and shoulder pads." Standing, he headed to the door by way of the kitchen table, pausing to give Lauren a quick kiss on the lips before moving on. "See you at eight?"

"I'll be ready."

So will I, he thought. So will I.

Chapter Seven

"Just one more, and then you two can leave."

"Promise?" Lauren asked. Diana, who took all the photos for the food section she edited, was really a very skilled photographer. After posing for half a dozen shots, however, Lauren felt wilted as a leaf of lettuce in one of the fancy salads big sis sometimes featured.

"I promise. Now let's do one of those traditional shots. You know...where the gangster is sitting straight as a rod in a chair, and his moll is standing behind."

Lauren grimaced. "His moll? Well, I like that!"

"So do I," Nick said even as he sat in the ladder-back chair Diana had dragged from the kitchen.

Hiding a smile at his comment, Lauren smoothed the red-and-black feather trim on the bodice and shoulders of her dress and moved behind the chair.

"Oh, that won't work," Diana commented with a moan. "I can't see your gown."

"By all means, get the gown," Nick said, swiveling clear around and, for the millionth time since his arrival, giving Lauren a once-over that made her blood boil.

Diana thought for a moment. "Sit in Nick's lap."

"*What?*"

Diana grinned. "Trust me. This is going to be great."

"Great," Nick echoed, his eyes twinkling with mischief.

Gingerly, Lauren sat on his lap. The skirt, slit to forever on the side, fell open, revealing a lacy black garter.

"Where do you want my hands?" Nick asked Diana.

"Where do you want to put them?" Diana retorted, laughing, an answer reminiscent of Nick's the first night he and Lauren had stretched out on her couch together.

Lauren guessed Nick remembered that night, too. At any rate he laughed and flexed his fingers as though about to grab hold of fully curved, slightly overexposed body parts.

"Do it and die," she said, twisting half around, shaking a finger at him. Diana's camera flashed.

"That, folks, was priceless."

"And that, sister dear, was the last one." With relief, Lauren slipped off Nick's lap and smoothed the dress. "You're sure this isn't too much?" The red satin garment clung to what curves it did not expose.

"You look fantastic."

"And you look deadly. Especially with that tommygun." She let her gaze caress Nick, beginning with the fedora, moving down the lean length of double-breasted pinstripe suit to the tips of his flashy, wing tip shoes. Man, oh man.

"It's a water pistol, actually."

"Thanks for the warning," Lauren said, taking his free hand, guiding him to the door. There, she turned to

Diana. "I suspect we'll be in very late ... barring any pages, that is." She patted Nick's coat pocket, where earlier she'd tucked her pager.

"Don't worry about me. As any mother can tell you, and as you will one day find out yourself, being alone is sometimes a real treat."

Diana's words stayed on Lauren's mind during the drive to Christopher Sanders's house. Moments alone might be appreciated by overworked mommies, but they were a drag for lonely doctors. Not that there hadn't been days when time alone was a precious treasure. There had ... before Nick walked into her life. Now Lauren preferred to be with him, the reason their conversation about life post-Diana had so pleased her.

It seemed there was a chance they'd spend time together as lovers. Good, Lauren thought with a quick smile at Nick, now braking the car at the black wrought iron gates at the end of Sanders's drive. Nodding at the gatekeeper, Nick drove onto his boss's property, but not before he picked up on the fact that she watched him. Turning his head, he intercepted her smile and gave her a devil-may-care grin that sent a wicked shiver right down her spine.

Lovers. Oh, yeah.

Never mind that she had no business wasting time on an affair when she should be looking for a husband. Nick would make the delay worthwhile by fulfilling a teenage fantasy and partnering her in some adult fun and games. In turn she would try to give him something too—a new self-image. Try as Lauren might, she could not understand why Nick thought of himself as uncommitted and undependable. Leftover lessons taught by a bitter father, perhaps? Those could be the hardest to shake.

As for Nick's complaint that he was always searching . . . who wasn't?

No, if there was anything wrong with the man Nick Gatewood had become, Lauren just couldn't see it. And more than ever she wanted to do right by him. That meant pointing out all the fire escapes in her life before letting him in the front door, so he'd know how to exit if things got too hot to bear.

"It's so nice to meet you," Lauren said for at least the millionth time an hour later. Her face ached from smiling. Her feet ached, as usual, from the heels she wore. To make matters worse, Nick had been abducted by Phillip Avery less than thirty minutes after they walked through the door, leaving her to her own devices. Luckily she had years of experience meeting strangers, so it was an irritation more than a problem.

The room buzzed with the separate conversations of her fellow guests, of which there were many. Lauren also heard the sound of music, barely discernible in the background. A glance at the decorations, predominantly black and orange in honor of the season, revealed them to be tasteful, clever and most likely the work of a pro. She marveled at the amount and variety of food spread on a table near the bar.

"So how does it feel to be the best-kept secret since the recipe for Coke?" asked the intense young architect just introduced as Alejandro by their hostess, who'd immediately vanished. Dressed as Zorro, he spoke with a Spanish accent that could not have been faked.

Only half listening to her companion, Lauren watched the door through which Phillip had dragged Nick. "I'm really not a secret at all."

"Oh, I think you are," Alejandro murmured, his dark-eyed gaze—all that she could see of his masked face besides his mouth and chin—sweeping her dress, lingering where it shouldn't. He reached out to tug one of the feathers on the shoulders of her dress, an action that caught Lauren off guard and made her flinch, embarrassing herself. "A secret weapon designed to sway the opinions of three very impressionable partners."

"Excuse me?" He had her full attention now.

"Don't tell me that you don't know."

Lauren hesitated. "Know what?"

"That I'm Nick's competition for the partner vacancy."

"Is there a vacancy?" Lauren murmured, feigning surprise. "I hadn't heard."

Alejandro chuckled his disbelief. "And this dress you're barely wearing isn't red, either, is it?"

His gaze swept her yet again. Suddenly uncomfortable with his look, with his attitude, Lauren stepped away and, smiling a cool dismissal, left, seeking the nearest fresh air just as she'd done at Phillip Avery's an eternity ago. Tonight it wasn't a garden, but an ornate wooden veranda that stretched the length of the house. Lauren reached it by exiting through double doors with French windows.

What was it about Nick's co-workers that made her long for the great outdoors? she wondered, wandering to the rail to look out over the moonlit lawn. More important, did Nick ever experience the same need?

It was hard to believe he didn't—which explained his apparent reluctance to consider the possible partnership in his company. But surely everyone wasn't as unpleasant as Zorro. Surely there were normal, nice people in that room.

Curious, she moved back to the door and peered casually through it, most likely invisible to those inside, thanks to the dark of night. No one looked normal—it *was* a costume party—but a lot of them looked nice. Why, then, did Nick appear so undecided? As far as Lauren could see, he was just one of the Avery, Sanders and Wright bunch, fitting in perfectly.

Or was he...?

Lauren frowned, recalling the past weeks' flash glimpses of the old Nick. What if they were peeks at the *true* Nick, instead? What if he played a part, as she sometimes did? Wouldn't that mean that what she saw might not be what she'd get?

But of course not... because she wasn't going to *get* him at all. At least not on a permanent basis. And why wasn't she? Because he deserved better.

Would he appreciate her sacrifice? Was sacrifice even necessary? Now in doubt as to Nick's true identity, Lauren simply couldn't say. She did know that something very like panic gripped her whenever she realized she might not have an excuse to keep emotional distance from him.

"So here's where you're hiding." It was Alejandro, materializing from nowhere thanks to his dark costume. He held a half-empty wineglass. "I'm glad I found you. We didn't finish our chat."

"I have nothing more to say."

"Well, I have something to say—something I hope you will share with your *fiancé*." He said the word as if he knew it was a lie. "I hear that you're a doctor. I'm not surprised since you're obviously bright. I also hear that you have a thriving practice and that only the very wealthy can afford your clinic."

Was that the reputation she had? Lauren's spirits sank lower than her shiny red shoes.

"You have friends in high places, which Nick undoubtedly thinks will make you the perfect wife for a partner at Avery, Sanders and Wright, not to mention the perfect foil for him, a man who is and has none of those things. But while Avery may be fooled into thinking he is now the best man for the job, the others are not so easily duped." Reaching out, Alejandro brushed aside a tendril of hair that had escaped from her French twist. "In other words, Dr. West, if your goal is marriage to a partner, you've picked the wrong architect. Care to reconsider?"

"She would not," Nick answered from somewhere in the shadows just as a stream of water hit Alejandro square in the face.

With a squeal of shock, Lauren jumped back. Alejandro, spewing, choking, lunged toward Nick, and the men began to grapple in the moonlight.

"Do something!" Lauren exclaimed to Phillip Avery, who watched in round-eyed astonishment but never moved. A patio chair tipped over as the men bumped against it. Nick's water gun clattered to the wooden deck. Alejandro's cape swirled. A quick glance through the double doors confirmed that a party guest inside had heard the noise and alerted everyone that something was amiss.

Desperate to break up the skirmish, Lauren snatched up the gun and aimed it at the architects, both mad as hell by now and actually throwing punches. Water shot from the gun, dousing both Nick and Alejandro. With a curse Nick snatched the toy and tossed it to the chair, providing just enough break in the action that Lauren was able to step between him and Alejandro.

"Stop it this minute!" she exclaimed, placing a hand on each of them, acting as a human spacer.

Nick shook off her touch. "I'm not letting that son of—"

"Please, Nicolas." She spun to face Nick, focusing all her peacemaking efforts on him. Her words cajoled, begging him not to lose his cool completely. Lauren could see how Nick struggled not to trounce Alejandro, and felt a surge of relief when he finally caught her waist and pulled her close to him, a sure sign that common sense had won out. "Are you okay?" she asked. "Do we need to leave?"

"But you can't leave," Phillip interjected, stepping forward. "My partners and I are going to make our announcement at ten, and I want you both to hear it." He glanced from Nick to Alejandro, who continued to eye each other somewhat threateningly. "As I recall, those first two doors there—" he pointed down the veranda "—open into guest bedrooms. I suggest you gentlemen find towels and dry off. Meanwhile, I'll escort Lauren to the telephone."

"Telephone?" she asked, easing out of Nick's embrace.

"You've been paged by your answering service," Nick told her. Though his eyes still glinted with anger, he had the grace to give her a sheepish shrug. "That's why I came out here looking for you."

"I hope it wasn't an emergency," Lauren snapped, turning to Phillip. Slipping her hand through the crook of his elbow, Lauren left Nick. Together she and Phillip walked inside, where they were met with the curious stares of the other guests.

Lauren, who knew they couldn't have seen much, ignored them, focusing all her attention on Phillip, who smooth talked his way through the crowded, noisy room to the hallway. He opened the first door on their right, which proved to be an office, and flipped on a brass table lamp.

"The phone is over there," he said, pointing to a desk.

"Thanks," Lauren murmured as she moved in that direction.

"May I bring you something to drink?"

"Oh, would you?"

"Of course. What'll it be?"

"Just water, please," she told him. "I need my wits about me tonight." The comment made Phillip grin. Lauren marveled that he wasn't upset by what she considered the childish behavior of the two men who had the best shot at partnership of his company. Must be a guy thing, she decided, not for the first time marveling that men measured worth so differently than women.

The page turned out to be a message to call a patient at home, which Lauren did. After explaining to the woman, a first-time "mom-to-be," about edema, a common problem during pregnancy, she advised her to elevate her feet and ankles, something she wished she could do herself, preferably at home. She'd had enough of this party and, until she sorted some things out, of Nick.

Five more minutes passed before Nick returned to the gala, looking little the worse for wear. Alejandro, or Alex, as Nick had called him, came back, too, but stayed across the room from them. Whether the two men talked while drying off, Lauren didn't know, but it was clear that Nick had calmed down.

Still perturbed by what had happened, she barely spoke to him. Nick had shocked her tonight. There was no denying it. He had proved what she suspected—that he was not the man he seemed to be, was not totally civilized—and what she had to figure out was whether she preferred the architect in the three-piece suit to the gangster in the double-breasted pinstripe.

Or did she even have a choice?

One hour later Phillip Avery, Christopher Sanders and Herman Wright finally made the first half of their big announcement—Phillip was the partner retiring. Nick would have been shocked had he not been taken aside by the man earlier that very night and warned. While glad he'd been prepared, he regretted the fact that he'd left Lauren alone, leaving her open to advances from the likes of Alex, a man he'd never had any use for and now thoroughly disliked.

As for the rest of the big announcement, it consisted of a promise to fill Avery's shoes by Christmas and a gracious invitation to visit him at the Colorado ski lodge he would soon call home. Nick was not surprised to hear that Sabrina was there already, getting their new home ready and taking private ski lessons. Nick pitied the unsuspecting instructor who'd signed her on. Poor guy....

At that moment Nick intercepted Lauren's gaze, stormy as a thunderhead. So she was still steamed about the fight with Alex, huh? Nick looked quickly away, sorry he'd upset her, but in a way glad she'd seen him at his worst. In truth, that little altercation had revealed the man he was better than all the adjectives in *Webster's*. And from the look on her face, he had surprised—no, shocked—her.

But what did she expect? Alex had *touched* her, for God's sake, and if the jerk had decided he wanted to kiss her, too, Lauren could never have stopped him. Assuming she'd wanted to. Nick, who'd heard every word Alex said, realized Lauren hadn't been given time to respond to the man's outrageous offer before Nick pulled the trigger of the water gun. He experienced again the stab of anger—or was it jealousy?—that had resulted in his attempt to trounce the architect.

Frowning, Nick searched the room for Alex, only then realizing that he himself was the object of more than one guest's speculation. Obviously everyone wondered who would replace Avery. He wondered himself...a sure sign he was nowhere near a decision as to what he'd do if the partnership really were offered to him. And from what Phillip had hinted, it would be.

Around ten forty-five, Nick asked Lauren if she were ready to leave and wasn't surprised when she gave him a curt nod. In seconds they said their goodbyes, using Diana as an excuse to escape from a party that would last well into the night. Though Nick guessed Lauren wanted nothing more than to go home, he detoured through the city park, now dark and empty except for some late-night joggers.

He braked the car, killed the engine, then turned to her. "Want to walk?"

"In these shoes?" she asked, clearly incredulous.

A glance at her feet, barely visible in the dark, told him why—strappy red shoes with very high heels. Knowing she wore shoes far more functional most days, he looked out the window, found a nearby bench and pointed to it. "Want to sit, then?"

"What I really want to do is go home." Her arms were crossed over her breasts. Her chin had a decidedly stubborn set to it.

"You'd rather fight where Diana can hear?"

"We're going to fight?" she asked.

"If that pout is anything to go by."

"I am not pouting!" she exclaimed, turning on him. The move revealed her shapely leg from hip to ankle, and it was all Nick could do not to stare. Damn, but she looked good tonight. And if he hadn't given in to his temper, hadn't fought Alex, she'd probably be in his arms right now.

And not belong there.

Nick sighed, knowing that prompt, which had undoubtedly come from his conscience, was true.

"And even if I were," she said, "I'd have the right. My God, Nick, what on earth were you thinking of tonight?"

"What can I say?" he asked. "I tried to warn you."

She frowned. "What are you talking about?"

"Me. I tried to tell you that I'm not what I appear to be."

"You told me you broke engagements and hearts. You said you were uncommitted and undependable—"

So she had been listening. And she still wanted him? Nick's heart took a flying leap of hope, then sank again. Maybe *before* the party, but certainly not now.

"Never once did you tell me that you have the temper of a spoiled three-year-old and the self-control to match!"

Nick's jaw dropped. "And just where would you be now if I hadn't stepped in?"

"It's not where *I'd* be, it's where *he'd* be—in traction. I'm perfectly capable of taking care of myself, and if you hadn't interfered, would have done it."

"So I'm not the only one with a temper?"

That got her. He could tell.

"N-no," she stammered. "But at least I had a reason."

"So did I . . . he was messing with my woman."

"Your—?" Clearly speechless with shock, Lauren suddenly clamped her mouth tightly shut and stared out the window. "Take me home, Nick. Now."

He started the car and left the park, mentally kicking himself. His woman? Had he really called her that? Where in blue blazes had it come from? He wasn't some mountain man defending his bride, nor was he a biker defending his chick. He was Nicolas Gatewood—civilized architect, levelheaded adult.

Like a fast-forwarded movie, the events of the night flashed on the screen of Nick's mind. He and Phillip stepped out of Sanders's study onto the veranda and heard again what Alex said to Lauren. Nick felt that deadly stab of what could only be jealousy and then saw red. The water gun, a prop that should have been harmless, was in his hand, fully loaded. On instinct, he raised, aimed and fired it.

Damn. What happened to "civilized"?

More important, what happened to "adult"?

In total silence they made the trip. Only after Nick turned the car into her drive and braked, did Lauren face him again.

"I am not your woman, Nick. You are not my man. We are *friends* who made the mistake of pretending to be engaged."

"I know that. I really do."

"Then why did you fight with Alejandro?"

Nick shrugged and stared straight ahead, at her garage. "He deserved it."

She huffed her scorn of that reply. "What, exactly, was his crime?"

Nick's jaw dropped as he shifted his gaze to include her. "Crime? Try crimes. The man is an idiot with no imagination. He constantly undermines my ideas and my efforts—''

"So this is a work thing? You two don't get along at the office?"

He gave his head a quick shake. "We may not like or respect each other, but we've always managed to get along before now."

"So what was the straw that broke your camel's back? Why did the two of you fight tonight of all nights?"

Nick hesitated, at once reluctant to tell her the truth. "He touched you."

"So this was a rescue?"

"Yes. He needs to keep his hands to himself."

"Which is exactly what I was about to tell him when you acted out." She sighed. "I've had years of practice handling difficult people. I know how."

"I realize that."

"Then why the rescue, Nick? Why the fight?"

Nick sat in silence, trying to think of a way to sugar-coat the truth he wasn't ready to confess and she wasn't ready to hear.

"Come on now...speak to me."

Damn it all.

"Nick!"

"I was jealous, okay?" he exploded. "I saw you two out there alone in the dark. I didn't like it."

She looked as shocked and baffled as he'd known she would. "But you have no reason or right to be jealous. Not only had I just met the man, whom I didn't even like, but this engagement is fake."

"You think I don't know that?" He struggled for an explanation. "You bring out the worst in me, Lauren. That's all I can say."

"Ditto for me. So far I've lied to my secretary, my sister and my mother. To make matters worse, I've begun to resent being on call all the time, and I'm having trouble concentrating at work."

"Well, look at me," Nick retorted. "All I can think about is jumping on my Harley and getting the hell out of Dallas. Will Many Horses's job offer is even beginning to sound good to me."

She flinched as if he'd hit her. "Your friend has a job for you?"

Well hell. Somehow Nick managed a casual shrug. "Maybe..."

"In Wyoming?"

"Yeah."

Though the only light in the car emanated from the dashboard, Nick could still see that Lauren paled. "Are you going to take it?"

"I don't know. It doesn't pay all that much. And I have, um, obligations...."

"Financial?"

"Personal."

"Such as?"

He shook his head, refusing without words to tell her that she was the reason he couldn't seriously consider a move west. How could he leave if there was a possibility—albeit very remote thanks to tonight—that they might be lovers?

"This stupid engagement isn't somehow to blame, is it?"

"How could it be?" he hedged, using a technique he'd learned from Lauren, herself.

"I don't know. I just..." She shook her head, clearly bemused. "Maybe it's time to break up."

"But I just said the engagement has nothing to do with anything," Nick said. "And besides, how can we *break* up, when we're not really *hooked* up?"

"Like this," she murmured, suddenly handing him the diamond ring.

Stunned, Nick could only stare at the ring without speaking. Only the sound of Lauren's door as she opened it penetrated his fog of bewilderment. At once he reached for his own door handle.

"Don't bother," she said.

So it was goodbye without a kiss, farewell without regret. And all because of a stupid temper tantrum that really hadn't hurt anyone.

Assuming that was why.

Nick couldn't be sure, and oddly hurt, he had to wonder if she'd been looking for an excuse—any excuse—to dump him all the time.

"Does this mean you're going to tell Diana the truth?" he asked.

Lauren hesitated, then seemed to come to a decision. "Yes. I can't have her planning a wedding that's never going to be. She has enough to do already." She climbed out of the car, then stooped so she could see him. "What about you? Are you going to tell all?"

"Might as well." He grimaced, picturing that fun scene. "It shouldn't be a surprise. I'm sure they're all wondering what a class act like you ever saw in a hoodlum like me."

Lauren flinched and started to respond, then obviously thought better of it. Without another word she shut the door and headed to the house, picking her way carefully across the lawn.

* * *

"You're sure home early," commented Diana the moment Lauren stepped into the house. A glass of milk in one hand, Oreos in the other, she stood in the foyer, clearly en route to the guest room from the kitchen.

"Yes." Lauren kicked off her shoes, sighing when her bare feet touched the carpeted floor. Unwilling to meet Diana's curious stare, she focused her attention on wiggling her toes to get the circulation going again.

"Is something wrong?"

Trust an older sister to be able to read minds.

"As a matter of fact, yes," Lauren told her. "Um . . . how do you feel tonight?"

"Great . . . why?" Diana was frowning now and looked decidedly suspicious.

"We need to talk."

At once Diana's gaze locked on Lauren's third finger, left hand. "Where's your ring?"

"In Nick's pocket."

"Oh God. Are you okay?"

"Fine," Lauren told her, adding, "really," when Diana's dubious expression revealed her doubt.

"Here," Diana said, thrusting her snacks at Lauren. "Something tells me you need these more than me."

Wordlessly, Lauren took the offering—a family-proved cure-all—and took a big bite of cookie. "Let's go to the kitchen," she said as she crunched on the chocolate and icing. "You can get more cookies and milk."

"Am I going to need them?" Diana asked, trailing Lauren down the hall.

"Yes. And while you get them, I'll decide exactly how I'm going to share what's been going on." Lauren stepped into the kitchen and headed for the bar, where she sat on a stool and rested her elbows on the counter.

"You can't just tell me the truth?" Diana asked as she opened the cookie jar and took out three Oreos.

"I could," Lauren told her. "But you'd never believe it."

"No?" Diana looked from her sister to the three cookies lying in her hand back to her sister. "Will three be enough?"

"Better make it six."

"Oh, my," big sis murmured, reaching back into the jar.

Chapter Eight

"So how do you feel about all this?" Diana asked, nearly an hour later. She and Lauren had moved from the kitchen a good thirty minutes ago and now sat on the couch in the den, cookie jar between them, plastic jug of milk within easy reach on the nearby coffee table.

"Relieved, more than anything, I think," Lauren admitted and then sipped her tumbler of milk.

"Really and truly?"

"Really and truly. Not only can I stop feeling guilty for lying to you, I can quit thinking about Nick all the time and focus on my practice again."

Diana's gaze narrowed slightly. "You think about him all the time?"

"Well, I *have* been . . . but only because we were engaged, I'm sure."

"You weren't engaged."

"Don't nitpick. You know what I mean."

Diana settled back into the cushions and crossed her arms over her chest, her gaze so steady that Lauren found it unsettling. "I believe you have feelings for Nick."

"Of course I do. So do you, for that matter."

She ignored Lauren's jibe. "Do you honestly think you can turn off all those feelings just like—" she snapped her fingers "—*that?*"

"What do you mean 'all those feelings'? I like the man. I wish him well. End of story."

"So you're not going to miss his calls?"

"He really didn't call me all that often."

"Or those little get-to-know-you-better dinners?"

"We just got together like that a few times. Nothing to get excited about. Nothing unforgettable."

"Or his hugs and kisses?"

Lauren didn't respond for a moment, unwilling to start lying now that she'd finally come clean. "Admittedly he stirred up a handful of dormant hormones, but my unrequited teenage crush on him is probably as much to blame for that as anything else."

Diana acknowledged with a slight smile her younger sister's offhanded admission that such *had* existed, after all. Throwing her hands out, palms upwards—the universal signal for *Beats the heck outta me!*—she murmured, "Then what's left to say besides 'Please, God, don't let me be pregnant when my little sister really does decide to walk down the aisle'?"

Lauren couldn't believe her good fortune. "That's it? You're letting me off so lightly after flat-out lying to you?"

"I am . . . but don't get excited yet," Diana said with a look Lauren couldn't quite decipher, a look that made her nervous. "Because no matter what you claim, I know your heart has been touched by Nick, and I don't think it's going to be as easy on you as it was on your big sister."

Diana's words proved prophetic, beginning the moment she boarded her plane Sunday morning. Tears filled Lauren's eyes, and, suddenly blue, she barely made it back to her car before she cried like a baby.

It's just because I wish she lived closer, Lauren told herself as she dodged traffic on the drive home from the airport. In truth she recognized the complexity of the real reason, which had as much to do with her goodbye to Nick as her goodbye to Diana.

Though Lauren would've welcomed a page that day, she received not one the rest of the morning or all afternoon—a miracle, considering she had first call! As a result she spent the hours cleaning house and hovering near the phone, which never rang.

It felt odd to be so totally alone again. Quite a contrast from her life while engaged to Nick, when she'd experienced a certain feeling of expectation and excitement at all times. She thought about calling him, then thought better of it, knowing she should keep the break clean.

This way, he could accept without reservations the job offered by his friend Will. It was the perfect answer, in Lauren's opinion, to Nick's workingman blues. If she called, he'd start wondering if she had regrets, which would undoubtedly lead to his thinking they might be lovers after all, something she knew he wanted as much as she did. Not only had they talked the possibility to death, she could read his body language like a book.

Body language . . . or body parts?

Both, Lauren realized, the next instant closing her mind to any and all further speculation about Nick's body.

To keep her thoughts clean, she drove to the store to purchase Halloween candy, something she'd meant to do for days, but hadn't. Lauren roamed the well-stocked aisles, intending to kill time. Unfortunately, everything she saw reminded her of Nick, from the barbecue grills to the art pencils.

She still managed to muster up some enthusiasm for the season, thanks to the Halloween decorations, candy and giant pumpkin that she bought. Fully intending to turn her front porch into a trick-or-treater's paradise, she headed home, only to receive a page that summoned her to the delivery room. Sighing through a promise to do it later, she jumped in her car and headed to the hospital for what proved to be the beginning of one wild Sunday night.

The next day at the clinic was no better, but Lauren still managed to leave a few minutes early. Once at home, she quickly changed into jeans and a flannel shirt, spread some newspaper on the bar, then set her pumpkin on it. The moment she picked up her carving knife, however, the doorbell rang, a sure indication Halloween had arrived before she was ready for it . . . as usual.

Throwing her hands up in exasperation, Lauren hurried to the front door. She opened it, her gaze lowered in expectation of a pint-size trick-or-treater, and saw, instead, a man's knees. Slowly she readjusted, raising her focus of attention over denim-encased thighs, tantalizing button fly, and a Hard Rock Café T-shirt to a sexy smile she knew all too well.

Nick! her heart sang even as her gaze found and locked with his. She said not a word in greeting, so thrilled was she to see him again.

"Hi," he said even as he hooked his thumbs through belt loops that she suspected had never known a belt.

"Hi." She positively gulped the word and then blushed with embarrassment. "I, um, didn't expect to see you again."

"Yeah, well, I just happened to be in the neighborhoo—" He broke off abruptly, dark eyes widening. "I hope that's not for me."

Puzzled, Lauren looked where he looked and realized she still clutched a razor-sharp carving knife. "Oh, no. I was working in the kitchen."

"In that case, may I come in for a second? I have something to say."

"Sure." She stepped back, allowing him to slip past into the foyer. "How are you at carving pumpkins?"

"Actually, that's a specialty of mine," he said, taking the knife as if he didn't quite trust her with it. "And I'm surprised it's not one of yours. *Dr.* West."

She just grinned, shook her head in denial and led the way to the kitchen, where the bright orange pumpkin waited. Nick walked from one side of the bar to the other, eyeing the wanna-be jack-o'-lantern, making a show of extending his arm and sticking up his thumb to get an artist's perspective. Lauren laughed. God, but it was wonderful to have him in her house again. She just hoped he was also about to be in her life again, too, and to hell with the consequences, wisdom or foolishness of it.

"Happy? Scary? Sad?"

"Hmm?" She murmured, floundering in a backwash of hopes and dreams.

"This little feller, here," Nick answered, patting the top of the rotund pumpkin. "How do you want him carved?"

"Happy," Lauren blurted. "He's very, very happy."

Nick tensed at that reply, and looking suddenly pensive, laid the knife down on the bar and turned to her. "I had to see you again."

"I'm glad you're here."

"I know we're not good for each other."

"Maybe not..."

"But I don't think I can live if I *never* get to hold you or kiss you again."

"Then by all means hold me," Lauren replied, stepping boldly forward and into his arms, which welcomed and then tightened around her.

"I've missed you something awful," he murmured into her hair.

Lauren let her cheek rest on his pounding heart for just a second before tipping her head back. "I've missed you, too. Now how about that kiss?"

Nick covered her lips with his by way of reply, action that spoke more eloquently than words. They kissed with the hunger of abstinence, and Lauren marveled that it had been mere hours and not weeks since the last time. But for all its intensity, this kiss was different from the others they had shared, and when Nick finally stepped away, she could only stare at him and wonder what it meant.

He just gave her a grin and picked up the knife again. "Happy, huh?"

"Yes."

Whistling, he cut a plug out of the top of the pumpkin, forming a lid to the hollow interior. After lifting it off by the stem, they each grabbed a spoon and began to scrape the inside clean of pulp and seeds.

"Have you talked lately with Will Many Horses?" Lauren asked as casually as possible.

"Last night, actually. I told him I was going to pass on the job for now."

"Really? Why?"

"I'm not sure I've done all I need to do here in Dallas."

Now that was a cryptic answer if she'd ever heard one. "I guess nothing has changed at your office?"

"Nope." Nick set to work carving two round eyes, a triangle-shaped nose and a mouth that stretched to forever in a toothy grin. "Got a candle to put inside it?"

"Yes." She found a big round one in the cabinet and set it inside the pumpkin, then handed Nick a box of matches. Together they walked to the front porch and they set it in full view of the street. Nick lit the candle and strolled out into the yard, from where he gave Lauren a thumbs-up. She immediately joined him there. "It's perfect. Now help me decorate the front door."

"You'd better be quick," Nick murmured, pointing to some trick-or-treaters, headed down the sidewalk in their direction.

With a soft *Yipes!* Lauren dashed indoors, Nick on her heels. They made short work of hanging a witch decoration on the door and two black cats in the window. Then chimes rang out, announcing their first visitors.

Grinning her pleasure, Lauren opened the door and passed out candy, all the while *oohing* and *ahhing* over the costumed children she found on her front porch.

Nick sat on the stairs nearby and watched her in action, his heart full to brimming with what just might be love for her. He could not be sure, of course, having never experienced that emotion before, but he couldn't imagine what else would make him feel this way.

He found it tricky dealing with a woman such as Lauren. He found it hard to figure out what to do about her. Leaving was out of the question, but if he stayed, wasn't there a chance he—and she—would later be sorry?

Almost certainly. Though sexually attuned to each other, they were nonetheless a mismatch in other—very important—ways. She'd grown up surrounded by a loving family. The amount of schooling he could claim. No skeletons hid in her closet, waiting to spring forth and shock the world, while past scrapes and skirmishes marred his memories and, most likely, all his records, military and other.

She was, as he'd once pointed out to her, a lamb. And while not anything so blatantly malicious as a big bad wolf, he *was* a black sheep, with a black sheep's inherent potential to rock her world.

So what was he doing there tonight? Why, stealing moments of her time, all that he would, could allow himself. A bona fide Sissy West addict, he planned to come around whenever he needed a fix in the form of her smile, her kiss, her touch. In turn, he'd be available anytime she needed him. Surely Lauren, who was sensible on a bad day, would agree this was the best way to handle their mutual desire.

"Oh, Nick," she called, summoning him from his thoughts with a wave of her hand. "Come here and meet Princess Jasmine."

Princess Who? Nick wondered even as he got to his feet and joined Lauren at the front door. A glance out on the porch revealed that a girl, who looked to be four years old or so to Nick, no judge of such, now stood at the door. Dressed in tiny blue harem pants and a satin, sequined vest, she batted her eyes at him and tossed her hair, straight and pale as corn silk.

Nick imagined that this was how Lauren had appeared at that age. Or was he glimpsing the future? Seeing what a daughter of hers would look like? His heart lurched at the idea.

"This is Holly," Lauren said as she grabbed his arm and pulled him ever closer. "She lives about two houses down that way." She pointed east. "Doesn't she look just like Princess Jasmine?"

"Yeah, uh, sure," Nick mumbled, a reply that earned him Holly's giggle.

"Don't you know Princess Jasmine?" the child asked, obviously not fooled for a minute.

Nick had to admit that he did not.

Holly heaved a sigh and rolled her expressive blue eyes, then shook her finger at him. "Then you need to come to my birthday party tomorrow." She reminded Nick of Shirley Temple—a precocious blend of youthful charm and grown-up words.

He couldn't help but laugh. "You're having a party?"

"Yes, and we're going to watch *Aladdin* because it's my favorite."

Vaguely the word rang a bell. Wasn't that the name of a classic children's book or something? He glanced to Lauren for help.

"The Disney movie," she prompted.

Oh, yeah. Released a few years ago to excellent reviews. He remembered reading about it. "Right. Of course. Thanks for the invitation. I'll, um, see what I can do." Nodding and smiling like one of the slaves in her palace, he backed away and returned to his spot on the stairs. From there he watched as he had before, while Lauren doled out candy to a never-ending stream of children. This time around, however, he saw in each and every one of them glimpses of a future he would never have.

The next hour ticked by in slow motion. His fragmented thoughts melded into a daydream starring Lauren and himself. He saw them as married, living together in her beautiful house, treating the neighborhood children to Halloween treats. Dressed as Lauren was in her oversize flannel shirt, which hung nearly to her knees, it was easy to imagine her pregnant with his baby. He tried the fatherhood feeling on for size. He liked it.

Reality struck like a punch to his gut, and he hurt. God, how he hurt. So he'd come there tonight to steal moments with Lauren, huh? So he'd thought they would be enough to satisfy him for a while, maybe forever.

Fool.

"Quick, blow out the candle and grab the pumpkin before anyone else rings the bell!" Lauren exclaimed, motioning him to his feet. She clutched the huge plastic bowl to her chest.

Nick glanced at his watch, which told him it was just eight o'clock, then got to his feet. "Isn't it early to close shop?"

"Not if you're out of candy," Lauren retorted, tipping the bowl so he could see inside—empty.

With a laugh he did as requested, then turned off the porch light and shut and locked the door.

"Whew!" Lauren set the empty bowl on a table by the door then moved to the den. "I lost count at ninety-five. Where did they all come from?"

Though she pretended disgust and exhaustion, Nick could see that her eyes sparkled with excitement. On impulse, he reached out and pulled her close, planting a big kiss on her mouth, rounded in an *O* of surprise.

"Mmm," Lauren murmured, quickly getting into the mood of the moment. She locked her fingers behind his neck and pressed her body close, all the while skimming her lips over his chin and jawline.

Though Nick knew he should find out exactly what she wanted from a relationship, for the moment the will to do it eluded him. Instead, he backed up until he reached the couch, taking Lauren with him, then sat on the arm of it. He spread his legs and tugged her between them, shivering when his lower body, so sensitized, so ready, met hers. It didn't help that Lauren wiggled and pressed closer, seductive movements probably meant to tease, judging from the way she smiled into his kiss.

He growled, warning her of the dangers.

She laughed and moved again, egging him on.

Grasping the hem of her flannel shirt, Nick pulled it up and over her head without unbuttoning a single button. As a result her hair caught and she had to squeal for him to stop. It took him two whole minutes to backtrack and untangle. It would've taken less had she not complicated things by trying to remove his shirt while he still worked on hers.

"This won't be easy," she gasped between kisses placed to his bare chest, his neck, his mouth.

"Why not?" he somehow found wits to ask, as he unsnapped her bra and tossed it on top of their shirts. He palmed the generous curves he revealed, tasted them, then reached for the buttons on her jeans. "We've both done this before." One button, two buttons, three . . .

She laughed then, a husky chuckle that turned him on even more, if that was possible. "I'm not talking about that, silly," she murmured even as she began to return the favor. One button . . . two. . . . When he moaned soft encouragement, she kissed his chest, just over his racing heart. "I'm talking about our affair. It will be tricky at times, and you may have to be patient, but I swear I'm going to work really hard to be available whenever you want me."

Impossible, Nick realized with certainty. He reached down and captured Lauren's fingers, now struggling with button number three, in his. "Before we go any further, I think we need to talk."

"You've got to be kidding," she murmured, laughing breathlessly. The next instant she seemed to take note of his serious expression, and her smile vanished. "You're serious."

"Yes." He scooped up her shirt, helped her slip back into it and buttoned a strategic button, during which she cooperated mechanically. And while she spoke not a word, her eyes—huge, accusing, questioning—communicated perfectly her sudden confusion.

His gaze everywhere but on her face, Nick led her around the arm of the couch to the front of it. They sat together.

"I'm listening," she prompted, when he didn't immediately speak.

Nick nodded and plunged ahead. "What are your expectations, Lauren? What do you want out of this?"

The question seemed to take her aback. "Companionship. Sex. Conversation. Moral support." She shrugged. "I realize we'll give and get all this on the run, but that's okay...maybe even for the best. Um, what do you want?'' She looked even more baffled now, he thought.

"The truth?" He wasn't sure she could handle it. Hell, he wasn't sure he knew what it was... beyond a nagging need that he'd barely acknowledged, much less formalized.

"I prefer it."

"When I came over here tonight, I was a man with a plan—a plan that matched yours."

"*Matched* past tense?"

So she'd picked up on that, huh? "Yeah."

"And now?"

"Now I find I want... more."

She frowned. "How much more are we talking here? A set Monday, Wednesday, Friday sort of arrangement? Every weekend?"

"Actually, I mean more, as in sharing a roof... for starters."

"Oh." Clearly startled, she thought about his words for a moment. Nick could tell the moment his idea began to appeal to her. "That would make life simpler, wouldn't it? I mean we'd save a lot of phone calls and road time." She smiled. "I believe I could handle cohabitation."

"It's not just cohabitation I want, Lauren."

"But you said—"

"'For starters.' I said 'for starters.'" Time for the hard part—a part he wasn't sure he could explain since he didn't understand it fully, himself.

Nick got to his feet and began to pace the room while Lauren watched, clearly bemused. No wonderful words came to him. He simply knew he needed a tie stronger than no-strings sex or temporary cohabitation to bind them. He needed legal assurance that he would be part of her future.

She huffed her exasperation. "For God's sake, Nick, just say it!"

"Okay...all right...I will." He stopped his march right in front of Lauren and, hands in his pockets, stared down at her. "I want to be the father of your children."

Chapter Nine

Lauren stared at Nick in astonishment, so shocked she couldn't breathe, much less speak. "But you know how I feel about parenting. I'm very traditional. *Very.*"

He nodded his apparent understanding of all that the word *traditional* entailed.

"Then that was a—" *Oh God* "—proposal?"

Again Nick nodded.

"I—I don't know what to say." Dazed and slightly dizzy, she got to her feet and walked straight to the kitchen, where she grabbed the cookie jar.

"What are you doing?" Nick asked from the doorway, bewilderment and possibly temper in his tone.

"I need an Oreo." Lauren dug into the jar out of blind reflex, her thoughts a whirlwind inside her head.

Nick stepped forward, took the jar away to slam it down on the counter—an action that successfully snapped her from her daze. "And I need an answer. Will you marry me, Lauren? A simple yes or no will do."

"There is no simple yes or no!" she exclaimed, suddenly angry. How dare he toss such a complicated issue in her lap and call it simple!

"Sure there is. *Yes* means I'll do as a husband and father. *No* means I won't."

"How can you be so dense, Nick? *No* doesn't necessarily have to mean you won't do as a husband and father. It could mean I'm not ready to get married. It could mean I think you deserve better. *It could mean I don't love you.*"

"Or all of the above?"

His tone said he'd received her message...loud and clear. "As a matter of fact, yes. All of the above."

"So your answer is *no.*"

"Of course it's *no.* Marriage is out of the question." Impulsively, perhaps a little desperately, she hooked her forefingers through his belt loops and tugged him, resisting every step, closer. "So why don't we forget it and give some serious thought to an affair, which is really much more practical for our present situations and our crazy life-styles?"

Nick looked down at Lauren for a moment, then surprised her by reaching down to loosen her fingers from his belt loops. "Not interested."

So much for seducing him. "But Nick—"

He just shook his head and exited the kitchen, rebuttoning his fly as he walked and scooping up his T-shirt when he reached the den. Lauren scurried after him, watching while he pulled the garment over his head.

"I—I've hurt your feelings, haven't I?" she stammered, dead certain he was about to exit her life—probably for good—and totally at a loss for how to stop him. "I swear I never meant to. It's just that marriage to me would take so much commitment—"

"And my track record is a little less than perfect?" He stood at the door now, haphazardly tucking his shirt into his jeans.

"That's not true."

"It is true, and the reason you know it is *because I told you.*" He reached for the doorknob, but wasn't fast enough. Lauren blocked it with her body.

"Listen to me, Nicolas Gatewood. The reason I won't consider marriage has nothing to do with you. It's me who's the problem. Me and my clinic...my schedule...my obligations...! You need a wife who can be there for you like your parents never were."

That stopped him cold. "So this is a pity thing?"

"No, of course not," she responded, ducking his line of vision, which threatened to pin her to the door. "I just believe you have a right to the traditional life you never had. Remember what Diana said about us the night of the costume party? Well, she was dead on. Marriage to me won't be traditional, Nick. Not by a long shot."

He followed her, turning and taking a step closer. "Have I complained about the way you handle your business?"

"No," she murmured, taking a matching step back.

"Have I once asked to be treated differently from other men?" Another step forward.

"No." Another step back.

"Did I ever demand that you make any kind of sacrifice for me?" He towered over her, his eyes flashing in anger, his feet still walking forward.

"No." The backs of her legs met an obstacle. Her gaze locked with Nick's, Lauren reached behind to grope out the shape of whatever blocked her path of escape.

"Then stop using that as an excuse!"

Her Queen Anne chair. With a soft "Oomph!" Lauren plopped down on it just as Nick pivoted and walked back to the door. She leapt to her feet and followed, reaching him just as he yanked open the door.

"So this is it?" she demanded, catching his arm at the elbow. "This is goodbye?"

"Yes."

"You're not being fair, Nick. You've caught me off guard, and now you won't forgive me for not having answers to questions I never dreamed you'd ask. Hell, I didn't even know you were coming over tonight. I thought Saturday's goodbye was our last."

"So did I."

"Yet you're here..."

"I wanted you."

"And I want you, too. Can't we just take it from there and forget all this forever-after nonsense?"

"Three hours ago, yes. Now, no."

Her heart sank, a sudden nosedive that left her feeling disoriented and slightly nauseous. "What on earth happened to change your mind?"

"Not a what, a who. That little girl...the princess...um, Holly." He shrugged, evidently as baffled as Lauren now was. "I saw that blond hair and those blue eyes, and all at once I knew what I'd be missing if I let you marry some other guy."

Incredulous, Lauren had to laugh. "That almost sounds like jealousy."

"You could call it that, I guess."

"But to be jealous, you have to love..." she ventured somewhat hesitantly... or was it hopefully? Love would change everything because in Lauren's experience love translated to commitment—the kind her own mother had, the kind Nick would need.

But he just shook his head by way of reply, a nonanswer that could've meant anything or nothing. "I have to go, Lauren."

So he didn't love her, yet he wanted her to promise "forever." How typical of a man—or was it just the ones she'd been lucky enough to care about who demanded her all but never gave her a reason to risk giving it. Sick of them all, she stepped back out of his way and leaned against the doorjamb, hugging herself—all the comfort she could expect that night or any other.

"I'm really sorry I came by," Nick murmured as he stepped out onto the porch. "I swear my intentions were good."

"Good for *you,* maybe," she replied, her tone as bitter as she suddenly felt. "I doubt very seriously that they were ever good for me."

That said, she shut the door in his face.

Lauren's accusing words echoed in Nick's head all the way home, so by the time he crawled into his bed alone, he'd given them lots of thought and knew she was right.

He'd gone to her house for one reason and one reason only—need. *His* need. Oh, sure, he'd smugly convinced himself it was her need, too, but that was nothing more than an egocentrical assumption he hadn't the guts to question too deeply.

As for the proposal...in a way, he could say the same for that, too, since it stemmed more from a self-centered panic about his future than any desire to make Lauren happy. He'd asked for her future, then acted as if she'd put his nose out of joint when she'd questioned his right to it.

Idiot.

No wonder she didn't want to marry him. Hell, he would've said no, too, if asked like that!

So what now? Well, first on his list was sending several dozen roses to Lauren, along with a handwritten apology for trying to barge back into her life. After that, he guessed he would knock his nose back in joint and apply it to the grindstone, something he owed his bosses.

Nick sighed and gave his pillow a punch he really deserved himself. Why was life so complicated? he asked himself as he settled his head back on it for the umpteenth time. Why did he introduce himself as Lauren's fiancé that Sunday so many weeks ago? For that matter, why did he ever speak to her in the first place?

If he'd just kept his mouth shut, he'd now be a happy man.

At once Nick laughed aloud, a sound that echoed strangely in the room.

Happy? Who was he trying to kid? Except for a few glorious moments during his teenage years, he'd been basically miserable from birth. It was only during the past weeks with Lauren that he'd known real happiness.

Nick suddenly tensed, then shivered, chilled by truth he could no longer deny....

Lauren was actually those glorious teenage moments, too.

Nick did exactly what he promised himself he would do that week—work, work, work—in an effort to generate enthusiasm for a craft he once loved. He believed he made progress, and so, it seemed, did his three bosses, who called him into their conference room on Friday, the fourth day of November, and offered him partnership.

As a result, when Nick walked to the parking deck that afternoon, he felt better than he had in years. He got into his car, intending to drive straight home and treat himself to pizza and a beer.

For that reason, no driver was more surprised than Nick when he suddenly changed lanes—not the safest of moves in rush-hour traffic—and exited the expressway miles earlier than he needed to. Baffled, he let his subconscious guide him and soon found himself in the vicinity of Lauren's clinic. A quick study of the parking lot out front revealed that her car was not on the premises. Nick turned in, anyway, then picked up his cellular phone and dialed the clinic number.

"The Women's Clinic. Lisa speaking."

"Hi, Lisa. It's Nick Gatewood, Dr. West's friend."

He heard a soft gasp that left him puzzled until she murmured, "I thought you two had argued or something."

"Why?"

"Because she's been in such a funk."

So Lauren wasn't doing any better than he was. "Hmm. Where is the good doctor?"

"At Dallas Medical West. Mrs. Chester is having her baby this afternoon."

"Do you think I could see Dr. West if I went over there?"

"Sure. Just have someone give her a message. Or, better yet, hang around the waiting room. You can get her attention when she brings the new baby to the window to meet its brothers, sisters, aunts, uncles and grandparents."

"She does that?"

"Always. She's very big on family."

Reluctant to intrude on the Chester family's privacy, Nick worried about Lisa's suggested approach to hooking up with Lauren. The moment he walked into the waiting room, however, he realized his presence would never be noticed. Huge, cluttered, it was temporary home to not one, but five families consisting, it appeared, of every one of the relatives Lisa had named plus a few cousins and friends.

Nick settled himself in a corner of the room and watched the curtained window where a nurse told him the doctors made their appearance. His thoughts were on Lauren, who'd be surprised, probably displeased to see him. He knew that, yet here he was, the proverbial bad penny, always turning up in her life.

But what else could he do? Having just made the most important decision of his career, he now had no one but Lauren to tell.

At that instant a nurse came out and spoke to one of the families. Nick heard "...a boy..." then they rose en masse and rushed to the window just in time to see the curtains sway and then part. A person—Lauren—dressed in scrubs from head to toe but sans mask stood there, holding the tiniest, ugliest baby Nick had ever seen.

He was on his feet in a flash, hoping to catch her eye, yet determined not to barge in on the Chester family's moment. Would she see him? Would she?

Even as he worried, Lauren's gaze found him. She registered no shock, but gave him a vivid smile and inclined her head ever so slightly to the precious bundle she held. Her face glowed with joy. Her very being radiated the victory of a new life.

Stunned by her beauty, he gave in to suddenly weak knees and sat back down in his chair. It was just like before. He wanted to experience this moment, himself, and not with just anyone. With Lauren, who now knew he was there. Would she act on the knowledge? Nick dared not guess. Instead, he worked to catch his breath, worked to recover from the déjà vu that had knocked him slightly off-balance.

Minutes ticked by—ten, fifteen, twenty. Nick's stomach knotted with uncertainty. His pride struggled with the possibility that she would not see him.

"Mr. Gatewood?" It was a woman, dressed in a white uniform.

He leapt to his feet, an action that caused several other occupants of the waiting room to laugh. Belatedly he realized they probably thought he was an expectant father. He didn't care.

"Yes?"

"Dr. West asked if she could meet you in the dining room in five minutes. She hasn't eaten all day."

"Tell her I'll be there," he replied, turning toward the exit. The next instant he spun back around. "Where is the dining room?"

"First floor, E wing," replied the smiling messenger before she disappeared through a door marked Staff Only.

In fact, fifteen more minutes passed before Lauren entered the dining room—just enough time for Nick to move through the food line and buy them each a catfish dinner. Dressed in street clothes now, she still looked radiant, and Nick treasured the fact that she walked into his arms when he stood to greet her.

"They named him Maximilian," she said when she released him.

"That's longer than the baby."

"Twenty-one inches."

"The name?"

"No, silly, the baby. Twenty-one inches, eight pounds four ounces."

Nick just grinned and pointed to the food.

"Oh, aren't you a dear?" she gushed, slipping into a chair, picking up a french fry.

A dear? He almost laughed, knowing she might not have been so generous had they met under other circumstances. As it was, her present euphoria worked to his advantage.

"Why are you here?"

The question caught Nick off guard. So she wasn't totally bombed on endorphins.

"They finally offered me the partnership. I wanted you to know."

"Oh, Nick. That's wonderful."

"I didn't take it."

"What?" She stared at him, clearly shocked, holding in her fingers another fry.

"I told them no. And then I quit."

The sliver of potato hit her plate, splashing ketchup on her blouse. With a whispered curse, Lauren began to dab at the stain with a napkin, an action she soon abandoned to stare at him. "I don't know what to say."

"Neither did they, at first," Nick admitted. "Finally, when they realized I meant it, they offered the partnership to Alex. He took it, of course, and will fit right in, which I'd never have done."

"Were they upset, do you think?"

Nick shrugged. "Mr. A. was disappointed, I think. As for the other two, they told me I was welcome to come back if I changed my mind." He chuckled. "As a lowly architect, of course. Not as a partner."

She'd begun eating again, her mind clearly not on her food. "And are you going to change your mind?"

"Nope. I'm going to work for Will Many Horses." He grinned, relishing the joy of sharing good news with a close friend. "Would you believe he hadn't even tried to find anyone else to fill the job? Seems he was that damn sure I'd change my mind and take it."

She just smiled, from all appearances not a bit surprised. "Tell me about the job. You haven't, you know."

"No? Will is forming a nonprofit organization to help low-income American Natives build affordable houses and a school. I'm going to be his architect."

"Lucky Will." Lauren propped her elbow beside her plate, then rested her chin in her palm. "Will you be moving, then?"

"Just as soon as I finish up my current projects at Avery, Sanders and Wright." Closely he watched her. Did she care?

Lauren gave nothing away. "Congratulations, Nick. I'm very proud for you."

"So you think I'm doing the right thing?" For some reason it mattered whether or not she did.

"I do."

"And you don't think I'm a coward for not committing to AS&W?"

She shook her head. "I think you're the bravest man I know. I also think I'm a little jealous. For all my big talk and wishful thinking about making a contribution to society, I'm not so sure I have the guts to really do it."

Lauren suddenly looked more beautiful than he'd ever seen her. Desire washed over him—desire that was more than lust for her body. He felt lust for her life, as well. He felt love. There was no mistaking the emotion this time. It consumed him from head to toe. It knotted in his belly, twisted his heart, brought tears to his eyes.

"Are you okay?"

God, was it that obvious? Nick swallowed hard. "Yeah, sure."

Lauren pushed her chair back and began to rise. Nick grabbed her arm, halting the move. When she arched an eyebrow at him in silent questioning, he cleared his throat and tried to find words to make her stay. "What are your plans for the rest of the evening?"

"Bath and bed."

"Could I talk you into a movie, instead?"

"I'm really not in the mood for a movie."

"Forget that, then. We'll go to the mall or the park or—I know!—a midnight ride on my Harley."

She shook her head, her eyes sad. "No, thanks."

Nick tensed. "Then how about we just sit here for a little longer. I'd like to explain about the mess I made of things on Halloween."

"Forget it," she murmured, standing. "*I* have." To his chagrin, she offered him her right hand, just as a stranger might do. "Goodbye, Nick. Thanks for dinner and for coming by to share your good news. I'd, um, wondered."

"No problem," he said, getting to his feet, too, taking her hand in his. He swayed forward, hoping for a kiss. She swayed back as much, eased her hand free of his, and, spinning on her heel, exited the room.

The next week and a half, Lauren stayed as busy as possible so she wouldn't think of Nick. Sometimes her strategy worked. Most times it did not.

More than once, she used her rare free moments to wonder if he'd finished up at the architectural firm. If he'd moved out West yet. She played over in her mind the circumstances of their last encounter, altering her responses and imagining new endings. And though her responses varied, the fantasy ending remained the same: riding off into the sunset with Nick. Regret immediately followed her daydream—regret so intense she actually considered calling Avery, Sanders and Wright to locate him.

She didn't, of course. What was the point? Even if they met again and actually replayed their final scene, Nick still would not love her. No, all that would change would be Lauren, who had set aside every personal goal and dream to step into a *supporting* role she'd tried on for size twice before.

There'd be no real love affair and certainly no wedding. What they would end up in was a situation where two people shared a roof and lived lives that intersected only when they crawled into bed together. She'd been there, done that, and didn't intend to try it again.

Smart, her decision not to track Nick, but one which impacted on Lauren's morale in a big way. She found herself struggling to muster enthusiasm for the day, a phenomenon that hit crisis point on November 15, a heavily booked Tuesday when Lauren woke up in the dumps and could find no way out. As a result she snapped at everyone from the paperboy to Lisa, who soon began to find excuses to run the other way whenever Lauren stepped into the front office.

At one o'clock, Lisa peeked into Lauren's private office and reported that her four-thirty appointment—the last of the day— had canceled. Lisa's smile said she was thrilled Dr. West would be leaving a little early. Lauren winced when she saw it and wished she could start the day over. Thank goodness she'd be out of there soon!

At three Lisa caught Lauren in the hall and, looking quite pensive, reported that a patient had called desperately needing to see Dr. West *today*. As a result, she'd given the patient the four-thirty slot. Since Lisa looked ready to dodge a punch, Lauren held her ready temper in check and just nodded agreement.

Muttering, "I'm so-o-o glad I'm a doctor," Lauren then headed to the next exam room for the first of the back-to-back appointments that took her right up to four o'clock. When she stopped in the hall outside room B to glance over the chart of her next patient, waiting inside, she heard raucous laughter out in the waiting room. Though curious, Lauren resisted the urge to check it out. No doubt one of the children who so often accompanied their mothers to the clinic had done something funny. It happened all the time.

She examined the patient in room B, then moved to rooms C and then D, before heading once more to room A, wherein waited her four-thirty appointment. Lauren noted there was no chart tucked in the holder on the outside of the closed door and, huffing her impatience, headed to the office to find Lisa, who sat at her desk.

"Where's the chart for room A?"

Lisa, looking rather flushed, leapt to her feet. "I gave it to Rosemary. She must've left it the exam room." Rosemary was the nurse who took vital signs and noted them on the patient's record.

"Okay," Lauren murmured, motioning for Lisa, who seemed to be standing at attention, to sit and take a load off. Turning, she headed back down the hall to room A, where she knocked politely on the door, then turned the knob and pushed it open. "Hi. How are y—Nick!"

And it was. Sitting on the rolling stool she usually sat on, he looked better than any man had a right to look.

At once, love for him—intense, eternal and undeniable—stole her breath and her pride. Lauren swallowed hard, not knowing why he was there, but vowing he would not leave until some things were said and settled between them.

Nick was on his feet in an instant, obviously a little unsure of himself, but smiling that smile. Lauren shut the door and flew into his arms. He hugged her hard, but didn't try for a kiss, no doubt remembering the last time. Luckily Lauren, who'd left her reservations in the hall, took up the slack and covered his mouth with hers.

What a kiss...the best ever. Positively wicked. She gasped for breath by the time they ended it—gasped, then kissed him again.

This one was slightly less frantic, though Nick did back her to the door and pin her there with the entire length of his body. Glory, what a feeling to be mouth to mouth, breasts to chest, thigh to thigh with him again. She moved her hands over his back and hips, wishing she could say the words he'd once fantasized saying—*take off your clothes and lie on the table*. Wouldn't she just love to teach *this* patient the facts of life?

"Does that door lock?" Nick asked, doing some manual exploration of his own. Clearly he read minds.

"No."

"Well, hell."

Laughing, she slipped from his embrace and stepped back to catch her breath again. It wasn't easy. Just that look in his eye was enough to make her weak. "I'm so glad to see you."

"I'd never have guessed," he admitted with a decidedly cocky smile. He took a step toward her. She threw out a hand, halting him.

"No more. I have to know why you're here."

"I'm here because there are things I must say to you. I wasn't sure you'd take my call."

Lauren sighed her regret that she'd given him cause to think that. "I wasn't very nice to you the last time we met, was I?"

"Only because I was such a jerk the time before that."

They exchanged a look. Nick shook his head. "I've made a lot of mistakes the past few weeks. I don't want to make another."

"Ditto for me."

"So you agree we should talk?"

"Yes, and the sooner the better."

Nick grimaced and shook his head. "I'm flying to Wyoming in two hours, and I won't be back until the twenty-third."

"That's eight days!" Lauren groaned, plopping suddenly down on the stool.

"Yeah. Maybe I could call Will and try to get him to change his meeting or something."

"What meeting?"

"With the board of his new organization—twelve very influential American Natives who have the same goal. I also have appointments with some land developers and builders. Just some preliminary stuff. I'll probably not be in the position officially until the first of next year."

Lauren winced. "I think you'd better catch your plane, Nick."

"But—"

"But nothing. I'll be here when you get back. We'll spend Thanksgiving together, or try to. I have first call that day."

He stood in silence for several long moments, clearly in a quandary. "Wish I'd phoned you a week ago."

"And I wish I'd called you. God only knows how many times I stared at the telephone, thinking about it."

He looked surprised to hear that. "And why didn't you?"

"Because I didn't know how you felt about me, didn't know what to say."

He grinned. "How do I feel about you? Why, I love you. What are you supposed to say? Just say you love me, too. *Please.*"

"I do, Nick. I do love you, too."

"And you'll marry me?"

"Of course."

They didn't hug. They didn't kiss. Instead, they just looked at each other until Nick reached over and got a Band-Aid from a box on the table. His face solemn, he opened it, peeled off the protective strips and then wrapped it around Lauren's finger where, just weeks ago, she'd worn his second-hand engagement ring.

"I'm not sure this has simplified anything," Lauren murmured, holding her hand up to survey the result of his labors.

"I'm damn sure it hasn't," Nick replied.

"But we'll work something out."

"I'll find a way for us to be together," he promised, finally reaching down to pull her into his embrace. "A way that will guarantee sex on a regular basis."

"I'm all for that." She sighed as they kissed.

It was with obvious regret that Nick finally stepped away. Taking a tissue from a dispenser mounted on the wall, he dabbed at a lipstick smear on her face. Laughing, she returned the favor. They then straightened their clothes and opened the door. Not surprisingly, several nurses and Lisa scattered.

"Play it cool," Lauren cautioned in a whisper as she escorted Nick back to the waiting room. Maybe the other patients would think he was a concerned dad-to-be or something.

Nick gave her a solemn nod of cooperation then headed straight to the exit, only to pause, smiling mischievously, and give everyone in the waiting room a big thumbs-up. Groaning with embarrassment, Lauren fled to her office, but not before she heard the sound of laughter and applause.

Chapter Ten

Lauren hummed as she brushed vegetable oil over the turkey she'd bought the day before. She rejoiced that she was alive, at home and in her kitchen. Most of all she rejoiced that Nick would be over in less than an hour. That more than made up for the fact that she wasn't with her mother, Diana and family in Houston watching the Thanksgiving preparade show on television.

She quit humming and closed her eyes, reliving the moment just over a week ago when she opened the door and found Nick in exam room A. If she lived to be a hundred, she'd never forget the thrill of seeing him again, of knowing that somehow everything would be okay.

Never mind that she still didn't know exactly how. Love would find a way. She just knew it. And if *it* didn't, Nick would.

He'd promised, after all, and today she refused to think beyond that.

Singing now—an old song about a Thanksgiving trip to Grandmother's house—Lauren washed her hands, then reached for the salt shaker. After salting the bird, the smallest she could find at the market, she wrapped it in foil, then set the pan in the preheated oven.

She next peeked at the dishes waiting to be baked later, traditional corn bread dressing and sweet potatoes among them. Nothing, she decided, was better than turkey and all the trimmings. All she needed now was her guest to help eat them.

On that very thought, the doorbell rang, and with a laugh of sheer glee, Lauren ran to the door and opened it wide.

"Hi, there," she said to Nick, now standing on her front porch with that smile she loved on his face, a shopping bag in his left hand and his right hand behind his back.

"Hi, yourself." He stepped into the house, pulling his right hand out from behind him as he did, then handed her a colorful bouquet of autumn flowers. "For you."

"Ooh, nice," she told him as she took them. "Thanks."

"You're welcome." He reached into his shirt pocket. "This is for you, too."

Lauren took his second surprise, a small, gift-wrapped box. "What's this?"

"A bribe from Will Many Horses."

"Now why would he need to bribe me?" she asked, eyeing the box with suspicion and the strangest knot— almost like fear—in her tummy.

"I'll tell you later. Right now I need a kiss."

"So do I, Nick, so do I."

They kissed tenderly, then moved together to the den, where Nick handed Lauren the shopping bag. "Dessert."

"Homemade?" she teased.

"It was made in someone's home, yes," he muttered, an answer that made her grin.

While Nick settled himself on the couch, she set down the shopping bag long enough to tear the wrapping from the box he'd called a bribe. Lifting off the lid, Lauren found a pair of silver and abalone earrings, obviously handcrafted and exquisite by anyone's standards.

"They're incredible," she murmured, holding one up to her earlobe.

"Made by Will's wife," Nick said, adding, "and so was the pie, which was a royal pain to bring home on the plane."

"I can imagine." A little taken aback by the generosity of these people who might be friends with Nick, but were strangers to her, Lauren didn't quite know what to say. "I'm overwhelmed. Please thank them for me. Better yet, I'll write them a note tonight."

Lauren handed Nick the remote control and headed to the kitchen, where she deposited the shopping bag on the bar, then found a vase, which she filled with water and the flowers. She set it on the dining table—today reduced to a table for two—where they would eat their holiday meal before walking back to the couch, from where Nick now watched the Macy's parade.

Putting the earrings out of her mind, Lauren joined him. Just as she sat, he reached out and pulled her close, not letting go until he'd orchestrated a move that put her astride his lap.

"Surely you don't want me to sit here?" she teased, nonetheless settling her tush on his muscled, denim-clad thighs.

"Actually, I do."

"But you can't see the parade."

"I'll catch it next year," he said and then kissed her. There was magic in his kiss, magic in the air. Cherishing it, Lauren parted her lips and welcomed him to deepen the contact. It felt so right. So-o-o right.

Beep . . . beep . . . beep . . .

"Don't tell me!"

"I can't believe this!"

They exchanged a look of utter exasperation, then Lauren slipped off his lap and, snatching the pager off the telephone table where she'd placed it earlier, read the number to call—the clinic answering service.

She phoned them, got her message and contacted the patient in question, a woman who wanted to know if it would be okay to drink "one teeny tiny glass of wine."

"No," Lauren told her and patiently described the possible effects of alcohol on unborn babies. After moaning and groaning the inconvenience of her pregnancy, the woman rang off. With a sigh Lauren walked back to Nick. "Now where were we?"

"You were lying here—" he patted the couch "—and I was on top of you."

Lauren bit back a laugh. "That's odd. I thought you were on bottom."

"Either way, baby," he said. "Either way."

She went to him then, sat close, and cuddled up, her head on his shoulder, her arms around his waist. "How was your trip?"

"Great. This job is exactly what I've been looking for."

"Do you have an official start date?"

She felt his sudden hesitation . . . a sort of tensing that made her tense, too. "Monday."

"Wow," Lauren murmured, sitting up and turning so she could see his face. She couldn't tell what he was thinking. "I thought you said the first of next year."

"That was the original plan."

"Is that why Will and his wife are bribing me? They think I'm going to rock the boat?"

"Not exactly."

"Then why?"

"Because they want you to move to Wyoming with me. They want you to work with American Natives. There's a physician shortage there, Lauren. You'd be making a contribution to medicine, something you've talked about since that first day we met at Texas Stadium."

It was one thing to dream about doing that. Quite another to actually do it. Faced with the actual opportunity, actual change in life-style, Lauren could only stare at Nick and swallow—once, very hard. "I just don't know. I mean, this is so sudden."

"I told you I'd find a way for us to be together."

"Yes, but I didn't think it would be this."

Nick frowned. "I'm open to suggestions. If you have an idea, spill it."

"I don't. I just—"

Beep . . . beep . . . beep . . .

"Be right back," Lauren murmured, gratefully getting to her feet and walking to the pager once again. As before, it was her answering service. And, as before, one telephone call to a patient took care of the page.

When she hung up the phone again, she smiled an apology at Nick, then escaped to the kitchen for a few seconds alone. She needed to think, to consider what could well be the only solution to their dilemma.

Did she dare quit her job, give up her house and move out West? The thought of taking such a risk scared her silly, and a million reasons not to do it assailed her. What if she didn't like the climate? The patients? The clinic? What if her new practice proved *more* hectic than less? And what if the rewards of helping the people didn't outweigh the increased stress?

"Are you okay?"

It was Nick, standing in the door, watching her think. She could tell by the look on his face that he knew she had problems with his idea. She could tell her hesitation bothered him.

"I'm fine. Just a little confused." She gave him a half smile, all she could manage. "I guess I'm a bigger coward than even I thought."

He joined her at the counter. "That's a normal reaction. I felt the same. But if you think about it, this is really the only way we can be together and have both our career needs met."

"But I have so much money invested in the clinic."

"You can sell your interest in it to some other doctor. Dallas must have hundreds who'd jump at the chance to buy into a setup like yours."

"But what about my house? I've signed a year's lease, and I have eight months left on it."

"Ever heard of subleasing?"

Damn, did he have an answer for everything? Abruptly Lauren changed the subject. "Speaking of housing, did you look for an apartment while you were out in Wyoming?" She reached up into the cabinet for a plastic tea tumbler.

"I did better than that. I've made an offer on a ranch. Should hear something by Saturday." He walked up behind her and slipped his arms around Lauren's waist, pulling her back against him, resting his chin on her head. Pointing out the window, just in front of them over the sink, he said, "You can see the mountains from our kitchen window. They're incredible."

Our kitchen window? Lauren suddenly found it hard to breathe. Things were moving too fast, way too fast. Career-impacting decisions such as this required a lot of thought. "I wish you'd waited to make an offer on the place. I mean, what if I don't like it?"

"You'll love it."

"But what if I don't? Isn't the purchase of a house a decision for two?"

"There was another buyer in the wings, Lauren, and, to be honest, I wasn't sure exactly when you'd be living there with me."

"When or if?"

He released her, stepping back so she could turn to face him. "This move is a lot to ask of you. I realize that, and I don't want to pressure you into anything."

"Telling me you intend to go out West whether or not I do isn't pressure?"

She could tell that got him. "I'm not telling you that...exactly. I'm saying I realize it may take time to work this out. I believe we can, though, if you're really for my making this career move."

"I am...was...am." She groaned and tossed the tumbler, still empty, into the sink. "All I want is for us to be together. Do we have to turn both our worlds upside down to do it?"

"Of course not," Nick retorted, voice dripping with sarcasm. "You can stay here forever. I'll head to

Wyoming now. We'll get married over the phone and take turns flying across the continent on the weekends for conjugal visits." He huffed his exasperation. "For a doctor, you're damned naive."

"And you're damned insulting!" As furious with him as with herself for being exactly what he said—naive—Lauren pivoted on her heel and strode through the dining room only to stop short when the sound of a tremendous crash filled the air.

With a gasp of fright, she ran to the window, Nick right behind. She saw that a car and a truck had met head-on, thanks to the blind curve, and fearing someone might be injured, she dashed through the den and out the front door.

Nick followed, his heart in his throat. Total chaos greeted them at the street. Neighbors filed from their homes. Traffic backed up. A horn wailed. Lauren headed straight for the smaller of the vehicles involved, a compact car that had sustained a lot of damage to the left front fender and door.

"Oh my God. I know her. She's a patient." Lauren tugged at the crushed door, which didn't budge. She turned at once to Nick, who stepped to her aid and manhandled it open. He then stepped back and watched while she ducked her head into the car and began to speak soothingly to the driver, who'd burst into tears.

"She's seems to be okay," Lauren told Nick a second later. "What about the people in the truck?"

Nick confirmed with a glance that the occupants of the other vehicle, now piling out of it, did not appear to be hurt. He reported this to Lauren.

"Good. Has someone called 911?"

"I will," said a woman, who then headed for a house across the street.

The next moments were a blur of activity. One neighbor directed traffic. Another took on the task of crowd control. Yet another saw after the needs of the other accident victims.

Nick, himself, stayed beside Lauren, who maintained professional cool beyond obvious agitation that she could not remember the accident victim's name or the reason she'd last visited the clinic. Full of pride, he watched Lauren minister to the woman, now fully awake and somewhat dazed, soothing her with gentle words, all the while keeping her right where she was.

She's a natural, he thought, heart brimming with love. She's in her element . . . at her best.

The sounds of sirens soon filled the air, and in minutes an ambulance and the police arrived. Nick noticed that the two paramedics deferred to Lauren, whom one of them recognized, and he breathed a sigh of relief when they finally got the woman out of her car and onto a litter.

In minutes the men loaded her into the ambulance, which sped away. Guessing Lauren would want to follow it to the hospital to ensure that her patient was all right, Nick stepped over to his car and unlocked the passenger door, then motioned her over. She slipped into the bucket seat with a grateful smile. He shut the door, then walked around to the driver's side and got in, too.

"I couldn't even tell them whether or not she was pregnant," she told Nick, the only words uttered on the drive to the hospital. Once there, Lauren darted inside to the information desk. Nick saw respect on the face of the nurse standing at the desk. He recognized admiration on the faces of the interns she passed as she headed to the emergency room. It seemed that everyone knew her, and from all indications, everyone liked her, too.

Did he have the right to drag her away? he suddenly wondered as he headed for a chair in the waiting room. Sure, she'd complained about her work, but that might've been fatigue talking—something he'd actually suggested himself. Couldn't she make a contribution to medicine here? And mightn't a simple move to a less-popular clinic be as therapeutic for her as a move to a less-populous state?

But of course.

So what now? he wondered. Head out West alone for his big adventure? The thought made him sick. Should he, then, stay in Dallas? Another bad idea, but one that looked better when he reminded himself that Lauren...his precious Lauren...would be constantly by his side.

He sighed and scooted down in the chair so he could rest his neck. With his legs stretched out in front of him and his eyes closed, Nick imagined life with Lauren, here in the "Big D." He pictured the two of them breakfasting in her kitchen, washing his car, loving in their bed.

Nice.

He then pictured himself, back at his office.

Not so nice, but bearable...if he had Lauren to come home to.

"Nick? Are you asleep?"

With a start Nick returned to the present and found Lauren standing over him, a smile on her face. She laughed when he blinked and looked around to get his bearings. *Had* he been asleep? Nick glanced at his watch, flushing when he realized two hours had vanished.

Lauren perched on the arm of the chair. "The patient, whose name is Cheryl Jackson and who is *not* pregnant, is fine thanks to her seat belt."

"And to you."

"Today I didn't do anything anyone wouldn't have done," she responded, getting to her feet, pulling him to his. They walked to the car. Nick drove them back home.

The smell of turkey filled the house. With a gasp of remembrance, she hurried to the kitchen, but just enough cooking time remained for the dressing, sweet potatoes, green beans and rolls. Nick hindered more than helped, hovering at her elbow, sneaking bites of everything as it cooked. Neither of them mentioned Wyoming and Nick's job and their unsolved dilemma. There would be time enough to argue about those later.

Assuming they'd argue. Lauren, inordinately depressed because she hadn't known the name or condition of the accident victim, had begun to recall just why she once complained about her job. She glanced toward the dining room, where Nick stood puzzling over what piece of her grandmother's silverware went where and how to fold the linen table napkins.

Her heart filled to bursting point with love. How thankful she was for him on this day meant for thanks. He'd brought sunshine into her life. He'd brought rain. He'd taught her how to treasure both. Could she now let him ride off into the colorful Western sunset . . . alone?

Lauren's anniversary clock chimed 1:30 just as they sat down to their late Thanksgiving meal. They ate, relishing every delicious bite, and talked about everything except what mattered most—their future. Not once did Lauren's beeper interrupt them. She told Nick it must be because all her patients were eating, too. He just gave her a smile that didn't reach his eyes.

When they finished eating, Lauren headed to the kitchen to Nick's shopping bag and the dessert he'd brought, which turned out to be a pie. Upon removing the dessert container from the bag, she spied several colorful envelopes lying under it—the kind that photographs and negatives were in when picked up at the developers.

Curious, Lauren abandoned the pie and sat on one of the stools at the bar. "What are these, Nick?"

"Hmm?" He stepped into the kitchen, their plates and dirty silverware in hand. "Oh, um, nothing really. Just some old pictures. I'd forgotten they were in there." He as good as tossed Lauren's good china into the sink and stepped to the bar, his hand outstretched for the photos.

Lauren shook her head and did not give them to him. "May I look at them?"

"I assure you there's nothing there you want to see." He appeared more than a little distressed, which only served to pique Lauren's determination to see the photos.

"Naked women?"

"Don't be ridiculous," he told her, his cheeks staining crimson.

"Naked men?"

"No."

"Naked Nick?"

"Wyoming," he growled. "The pictures are of Wyoming. I took them this last trip out."

No wonder he didn't want to share. He, too, had enjoyed this past hour of peace and didn't want to jeopardize it.

Lauren patted the bar stool next to hers. "Sit. I may have questions."

With a groan, Nick gave in to the inevitable and obeyed. Lauren began to flip through the photos in the first envelope.

They were spectacular. Full-color shots of the mountains and valleys, the rivers, the flowers and trees. In spite of herself, Lauren thrilled to the majesty of the land.

Wordlessly she put the pictures back in their envelope and reached for the next batch. These were of buildings—houses that were really nothing more than shacks, a medical clinic that would fit in the waiting room of the one she worked in now. A general store, a gas station, a church. They tugged at her heart. They called her name.

With a gulp and a glance at Nick, who sat solemn as a church mouse, Lauren tucked the photos into their envelope and reached for the last set. With one glance at the first shot, that of a little boy with his front tooth missing, Lauren suspected she was a goner. The next picture cinched it. A young woman, obviously poor but positively glowing, tucked her dress under her bulging middle to accentuate her advanced pregnancy.

Stunned, trembling, Lauren barely saw the others, which were also of Nick's new friends. The last photo in the bunch was not of a person, but what looked to be a ranch, nestled on the side of a mountain. Instinctively Lauren knew this was the spread on which Nick had made an offer. She also knew that if she'd seen it first, she'd have done the same thing—whether or not he was along.

So this was the reason for his euphoria—this land, these people, this ranch. He'd found himself a challenge, a niche. Was it her challenge, her niche, too?

Yeesss! She knew it as surely as she knew she was born to be a doctor.

Swallowing back the lump of joy in her throat, Lauren turned the photo of Nick's ranch so he could see it.

"Ours?" she asked.

"About the ranch," Nick began, clearly ill at ease. "I realize now that I was selfish—"

"Is this *ours,* Nicolas?" She placed emphasis on the *ours,* knowing that he hadn't really heard it, waiting for him to.

"Saturday. I'll know by Saturday whether or not it's ou—" He tensed. "Ours? Did you say *ours?*"

Lauren nodded.

"Does this mean . . . ?"

She nodded again. "I have to go. I do."

"But you don't," he said, taking both her hands in his. "I'll stay here and get my old job back or get another. I'll do anything, everything to make you happy."

"That sounded remarkably like commitment." Lauren could not resist teasing.

He shrugged. "What can I say? All it took was the right woman . . . just what you once told me."

"Well, this right woman wants to accompany this right man to their right home." She pointed to the photograph.

"Are you sure?" He was on his feet now.

She stood, too, and slipped her arms around his waist. "Never more so. Are *you?* I mean, there are going to be times when you'll have to share me."

"I can handle it."

"You say that now, but what if we're in the middle of the most incredible sex of your life?"

"I'm telling you, I can handle anything. I'm committed." He placed a kiss on her lips as if to seal the promise. "I think we should celebrate this momentous occasion with dessert."

"So do I," she said, turning to the bar. "What is it . . . chocolate?"

"Oh, not that dessert," Nick told her with a shake of his head. "This one." He kissed her again, a hungry kiss that promised sweet pleasure.

"Yes," she breathed, savoring the treat. By mutual, unspoken agreement, they headed out of the kitchen and down the hall—destination the stairs, the bedroom, the bed.

Beep...beep...beep...

"Aww man! Already?"

*   *   *   *   *

Bestselling Author
LINDA TURNER

Continues the twelve-book series—FORTUNE'S CHILDREN—
in **November 1996** with Book Five

THE WOLF AND THE DOVE

Adventurous pilot Rachel Fortune and traditional Native American
doctor Luke Greywolf set sparks off each other the minute they met.
But widower Luke was tormented by guilt and vowed never to love
again. Could tempting Rachel heal Luke's wounded heart so they
could share a future of happily ever after?

MEET THE FORTUNES—a family whose legacy is greater than riche:
Because where there's a will…there's a *wedding!*

*A CASTING CALL TO
ALL FORTUNE'S CHILDREN FANS!*
If you are truly fortunate,
you may win a trip to
Los Angeles to audition for
Wheel of Fortune®. Look for
details in all retail Fortune's Children titles!

He's able to change a diaper in three seconds flat.
And melt an unsuspecting heart even quicker.
But changing his mind about marriage might take some doing!
He's more than a man...
He's a **FABULOUS FATHER!**

****

Cuddle up this winter with these handsome hunks:

October:

INTRODUCING DADDY by Alaina Hawthorne (RS#1180)
He just discovered his soon-to-be ex-wife "forgot" to
tell him he's a daddy!

November:

DESPERATELY SEEKING DADDY by Arlene James (RS#1186)
Three little kids advertise for a father—and a husband for
their beautiful single mom....

December:

MERRY CHRISTMAS, DADDY by Susan Meier (RS#1192)
A bachelor fumbles with rattles and baby pins—and his love for
a woman—all in time for Christmas!

January:

MAD FOR THE DAD by Terry Essig (RS#1198)
Overwhelmed by his new daddy responsibilities, he needs a
little help from his pretty neighbor....

***

Celebrate fatherhood—and love!—every month.
ABULOUS FATHERS...only in Silhouette ROMANCE™

Add a double dash of romance to your
festivities this holiday season
with two great stories in

Christmas
Celebration

Featuring full-length stories by bestselling authors

Kasey Michaels
Anne McAllister

These heartwarming stories of love triumphing
against the odds are sure to add some extra
Christmas cheer to your holiday season. And this
distinctive collection features **two full-length novels**
making it the perfect gift at great value—for
yourself or a friend!

Available this December at your favorite retail outlet

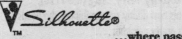

...*where passion lives.*

This holiday season,
Linda Varner brings three very special couples

HOME
FOR THE HOLIDAYS

where they discover the joy of love and family—
and the wonder of wedded bliss.

❄❄❄❄❄❄❄❄❄❄❄❄❄❄❄❄❄❄❄❄❄❄❄❄❄❄❄❄❄

WON'T YOU BE MY HUSBAND?—Lauren West and
Nick Gatewood never expected their family and friends to get
word of their temporary engagement and nonintended nuptials. Or
to find themselves falling in love with each other. Is that a *real*
wedding they're planning over Thanksgiving dinner?
(SR#1188, 11/96)

MISTLETOE BRIDE—There was plenty of room at Dani Sellica's
Colorado ranch for stranded holiday guests Ryan Given and his
young son. Until the mistletoe incident! Christmas morning brought
presents from ol' Saint Nick…but would it also bring wedding bells?
(SR#1193, 12/96)

NEW YEAR'S WIFE—Eight years after Tyler Jordan and
Julie McCrae shared a passionate kiss at the stroke of midnight,
Tyler is back and Julie is certain he doesn't fit into her plans for
wedded bliss. But does his plan to prove her wrong include a lifetime
of New Year's kisses? (SR#1200, 1/97)

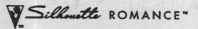

Silhouette ROMANCE™

The collection of the year!
NEW YORK TIMES BESTSELLING AUTHORS

Linda Lael Miller
Wild About Harry

Janet Dailey
Sweet Promise

Elizabeth Lowell
Reckless Love

Penny Jordan
Love's Choices

and featuring
Nora Roberts
The Calhoun Women

This special trade-size edition features four of the wildly
popular titles in the Calhoun miniseries together in
one volume—a true collector's item!

Pick up these great authors and a chance to win
a weekend for two in New York City at the
Marriott Marquis Hotel on Broadway! We'll pay
for your flight, your hotel—even a Broadway show!

Available in December at your favorite retail outlet.

NEW YORK
Marriott.
MARQUIS

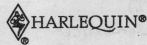

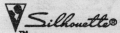